The Journey
Through Eternity

"In this opening volume of a trilogy, Fr. Bill Robinson brings contemporary characters into vivid dialogue with the great figures of the Old Testament. Far from treating these ancient persons as distant relics, he reveals them as living voices who remind us that Sacred Scripture is not merely ancient history—it is our own story as people of faith."

—ROBERT REED
The CatholicTV Network

"Fr. Bill Robinson has offered us a creative, imaginative, and refreshing tour through the Bible and our history of salvation. Readers will not soon forget Julia and Justin who guide us on our way, nor the biblical characters who come to life on these pages."

—JOHN F. BALDOVIN
SJ, Professor of Historical and Liturgical Theology, Boston College

"Imagine being an eyewitness to the major events of salvation history. Imagine eavesdropping on the most consequential conversations and conversions in the Bible. In the spirit of *The Shack* and *The Chosen*, and in a captivating and delightful way, Fr. Robinson brings fresh, vivid, and profound insights into the Greatest Story Ever Told. You will gain a deeper and more personal experience of God, the Scriptures, and eternity in your reading of this modern-day classic."

—RICHARD M. ERIKSON
Chaplain, Brigadier General, USAF, Retired

"Fr. Bill Robinson has had the intriguing idea of placing two contemporary young people, who are not certain of their own identity and origins, within the story of salvation history: in this first volume from Adam and Eve in Eden through the covenant with Abraham, the exodus and the Davidic kingdom. They come to engage personally with the great figures of the Old Testament and have a privileged perspective on God's action on behalf of his people. In so doing, they come to learn more about God's purpose in the world and in human history, and of their own identity and role in that purpose. This work should make the stories of the Hebrew Bible more accessible to young people today."

—JEFFREY VON ARX
SJ, Visiting Professor of the History of Christianity, Boston College

The Journey Through Eternity

NOVELLA I

William H. Robinson

RESOURCE *Publications* · Eugene, Oregon

Resource Publications
An Imprint of Wipf and Stock Publishers
199 W. 8th Ave., Suite 3
Eugene, OR 97401

www.wipfandstock.com

PAPERBACK ISBN: 979-8-3852-6649-4
HARDCOVER ISBN: 979-8-3852-6650-0
EBOOK ISBN: 979-8-3852-6651-7

VERSION NUMBER 012126

CONTENTS

AUTHOR'S NOTE

In what follows, some of the speech from God, an angel of the Lord, Moses, and Solomon, along with a song of praise from Moses and the Israelites, is drawn from the New American Bible, revised edition.

Chapter One

THE UNEXPECTED

JUSTIN KEPT HIS EYES shut tight, for it seemed that he was given a reprieve from whatever was about to happen. Only moments ago, he was filled with uncertainty, or better said, even a sense of despair at whatever he was, or was not, about to do. Yet, in the mere seconds he had been standing wherever he was, the winds of serenity began to fill him.

He decided to chance it, and upon opening his eyes he was not disappointed. He found himself surrounded by a forest of deep green pine trees, crimson red maples, and snow-white birches.

Taking a breath of the cool and fresh balsam-scented air, he felt the tension continue to melt away. As he stood there, he found that this place was peaceful, beautiful, and pristine.

After a time, Justin heard a voice behind him say, "Hello, are you from around here?" Her voice was sweet and in turning to her he could see that there was a definite loveliness about her. For a moment his eyes met with hers, and he felt a connection with her, even though he could not find a single memory of her in his mind.

"I'm Julia," she said as she gave a half smile and held out her hand.

"I'm Justin," said Justin who shook her hand.

Julia went on, "I take it that you have the same questions as I do?"

At that Justin smirked and said, "I don't know if I can even begin to explain all the questions I have."

Justin didn't know which peculiarity he wanted to voice initially, for there were many. The first peculiarity was that he did not know where he had come from, nor could he remember what had happened prior. It was strange. He found that he retained his general knowledge and skill sets, but he did not know who he was nor did he have details of his personal life.

The second oddity was related. Even though he retained such wisdom and skill sets, there was much knowledge that he felt wasn't present.

The list of his questions was long, but he decided to address these two first and thus explained to Julia his predicament. To his surprise, and to his relief, Julia said she was in the same state as he.

And then Julia laughed, to which Justin joined in. Whether it was a laugh of relief or of the sheer craziness of the content of their conversation, Justin did not care, for it was a time of laughter that Justin hadn't felt in some time.

"So, we have been transported to an unknown forest, and have no idea what is going on, nothing weird about this at all," she said with a smirk. After another bit of smile and laugh, Julia then asked, "Well let's check this place out, shall we?"

At that, Julia set off, and he began to follow. As they walked around the pine forest, Justin recognized that this place exuded extra joy and comfort. In fact, now that he had been there and broken the ice with Julia, he found it to be a realm that was clearly a "cut above" anywhere he had ever been.

Then, nestled within the trees, Justin spied a picture-perfect country log cabin, complete with a quietly smoking chimney. It displayed a deep friendliness and was most inviting.

Yet, it was *who* was at the entrance that really caught his eyes. There, at the doorway, stood the most beautiful woman he'd ever seen. She wore a gorgeous white mantle edged with gold and a garment of deepest blue edged with silver. She wore a crown of silver on her head, upon which were twelve shining stars. Her face was pure and sweet, her eyes piercing but lovingly blue. What was her age? The answer was hard for Justin to pin down. At one and the same time she was young, youthful, and beautiful beyond imagining. Yet, she was also solemn, wise, courageous, and had a beauty of depth. She displayed a purity beyond even the whitest new-fallen snow.

The lady smiled and motioned for them to come to her. With twinkling eyes, she ushered them in. Inside the log cabin was just as cozy and pastoral as it looked outside. As he walked inside he came into a grand room that was an ornate library. It was a large rectangular area and a lightly pitched roof. A plush rug of blue covered the floor. Open windows looked upon the field and forest and took in the pine-scented air.

All the walls were covered with dark brown wooden bookshelves carrying a multitude of books, save only where the windows were. While the room had a powerful effect, it still had the country charm of a log cabin.

A fireplace with a crackling fire occupied one end of the room. From it drifted a rustic smell of smoke; no campfire could have smelled better. In the center of the room was a table made of mahogany wood which matched the color of the walls and roof. The table was complete with chairs and tea was set for three. In the center of the table was the most vibrant vase of red roses, and their fragrance Justin could only describe as love.

As Justin's eyes continued to fall upon the place, he saw some doorways which he assumed led to a dining room, bedrooms, etc.

Turning back towards the table set with tea, the lady, Justin, and Julia sat down together. "My name is Mary," said the lady with a smile. Justin felt a familiarity in her presence but could not articulate what that meant or who she was.

Justin simply sat back, taking in this amazing turn of events. After a few sips of tea, Julia spoke and asked, "Mary, what *is* all of this?"

After a pause, Mary smiled and explained, "Justin and Julia, you have been brought here in answer to the prayers of others, and prayers of admittedly utmost importance. To answer these prayers, I will take you on a journey, a journey through eternity."

At these words Justin found he could add two other peculiarities to his list, which were thus: he could not remember much of anything about God and religion beyond just a vague concept, and he could not recite basic world history. He was surprised, but eased, when it was Julia who put such concerns into words to Mary.

Mary smiled and answered, "You now have the ability to ask questions and a freshness that most people long for. In a sense, you are that much closer to being able to experience faith 'like a child.' Cherish this time and enjoy the gift of being able to learn again anew. To experience the whole idea of God and history for the first time, again, is a great gift, which is what you both shall have."

It was funny, Justin would think that such a condition would give him cause for concern. While he certainly did feel some trepidation, the idea that he could have another "first chance" was like a warm light that dispelled any unease that he had.

Mary was silent as she let this sink in and then continued, "Now let us get back to your journey." Before Justin could open his mouth and ask all of the logistical questions of such a journey, Mary, with a look of understanding in her eyes, gave some explanation.

"You will experience spiritual and physical history as it really is, however, some parts of the journey will be symbolic, some literal, and some will be a mix of both. Regardless of their type, they will all be *real*.

Whenever and wherever you go, you will fit in naturally, and those with whom you interact will know you as appropriate. Everything will be colloquially in language you understand, and dates used will be according to the system you know."

Gesturing to the many books on the library shelves Mary went on, "It is through these books that you will indeed find yourself in each place and time. The books are ordered by their 'time' in history. Earlier in history is to the left side of the library and later in history is to the right. Once there, you will experience your reason for being there and all of the graces and wisdom that will come with it."

After a pause, Julia asked, "How do we get back from where we have gone?"

Mary answered, "Once your mission and reason for being where you are has come to an end, the book you used to transport yourself will present itself, and upon opening it you will find yourself back in this library."

"If I may," continued Mary. "Let me suggest you begin with the book entitled *Creation* as a good starting point."

"Wait," said Justin who went on, "look, I am all for checking out creation, but, we need to at least know *something* about who we are." Glancing at Julia he was ratified to see a longing in her eyes as she, like him, stared back at Mary awaiting a response.

Mary, in a light but deliberate tone, answered, "Ah let's see, yes, this is significant, you are both seventeen and both lifeguards at the same park, a lovely lake, surrounded by pines, with snow-capped mountains in the background. A meaningful age and place for you both."

Without elaboration, Mary went to the bookshelves and picked up a book, not from the farthest left, but near the right end of the left wall. Apparently, there was a large number of books about what took place "before" creation.

After picking out the book entitled *Creation*, Mary handed it to Justin. "Before you experience the creation of your world, there will be one visit first, a visit to the Divine." Mary then took her leave, stepping out into the forest outside.

Justin was conflicted. At one and the same time he felt a great hope that whatever this venture was would make all things well. However, he also felt a wave of gravity was upon him, for he felt that the outcome of whatever this journey would be was imperative to not only his life but even to many others as well. As he watched Julia, he could see that she must be having similar thoughts.

"Well?" asked Julia. "I guess there is nothing to do but give this a whirl. I mean, all we are going to do is meet God, take a journey that our lives depend on, and see if whatever religion we are about to experience actually has real validity or not." Justin couldn't tell whether her tone was sarcasm or wit. However, he was sure he saw a small gleam in her eyes. In any case, Justin nodded, opened the book entitled *Creation*, and the scene dissolved.

Chapter Two

HAPPINESS

NOT THAT JULIA KNEW what to expect—she had never met God before—yet she was surprised when she found herself, still side by side with Justin, inside a pine woodland at the edge of a small bubbling brook. In fact, it looked exactly like the same forest that they were already in.

As Julia looked around, all that was in front of her was a small wooden bridge that crossed the brook. Other than that, it was just a nice bit of nature. "Let's cross the bridge and see what there is to see," offered Justin. After crossing the brook, the forest opened to a clearing with perfect plush green grass and a smiling sun shining overhead.

And then Julia and Justin stopped in their tracks, for there in the center of the clearing were three persons whose magnificence was beyond description.

Each emitted the pinnacle of grandeur. Their faces were like the appearance of a rainbow in the clouds, and brilliance itself surrounded them. At one and the same time, each possessed endless wisdom and infinite youth. Immense power could be felt, yet, at the same time, their features were as gentle as the buttercup flowers blowing softly at their feet.

As Julia stood there with Justin at her side, she felt a sense of reverence that she had never felt before. The first person was dressed in garments of forest green lined with gold and wore a crown of twinkling emeralds. The second person was dressed in garments of crystal white lined with gold and wore a crown of sparkling diamonds. The third person was dressed in crimson red lined with gold and wore a crown of glittering rubies.

As Julia remained immersed in their beauty, she saw a brilliant ray of light radiate from them. It seemed to Julia as if it was a thought, an imagining, a vision willingly and happily put forth. This thought took the form of a gorgeous rainbow. In the middle of it, between the yellows and the greens, were the colors of silver and gold.

This rainbow, for a moment, swayed in the sky, and then turned in Julia's and Justin's direction.

As the rainbow reached her and Justin, with the feel of a gentle wind, the rainbow picked them up from the soft grass they were standing on. Then it took them, not just out of the knoll they were in but wholly out of their current realm.

While still upon the rainbow, Julia found herself in what only could be called a void. All was dark and quiet. There was nothing. After a pause, the rainbow carrying her burst into countless threads of glittering color which gushed forth in every direction.

As the threads of colored light pranced all around, the surroundings changed from nothing into something. The first thing Julia noticed was that she and Justin were no longer in darkness or in a void, but she could now presently ascertain the stars and the vastness of space.

It was like being among the stars and seeing the great images of the Hubble and Webb Telescopes all at once. She saw the constellations as she had never seen them—the majestic figure of Orion, the soaring Pegasus, and the young maiden Virgo. She saw glowing nebulas giving birth to stars and breathtaking spiral galaxies spinning like flashing pinwheels.

Mesmerized by such a sight, she came to notice that her footing became steady upon a solid surface. Now before her lay a vast land of rich black earth, white sands, and gray granite. Meeting her ears came the sounds of bubbling, sounds which found their birth at lakes, rivers, and springs.

As she surveyed the land it became day as a yellow-white light beamed down from a youthful sun whose radiance filled her eyes and heart. Filling in around her was fresh, spring-scented green grass and tall oaks with leaves edged with silver. There were bushes of blueberries, strawberries, and bright corn. Julia could almost taste their perfect flavor just by smelling their sweet aromas.

Then, prancing upon the lush green grass was a family of young deer covered with brown fur and white spots. Cheerful gray squirrels darted up and down the trees in play. Overhead, birds of all sorts flew: royal red cardinals, blue jays, and golden finches, all singing a song the rest of creation listened to with pleasure. She also spotted cats, bears, dogs, and countless others.

After the appearance of the animals, she noticed a special joy resonate throughout the land, and the word "good" seemed to echo across the air. As she surveyed the whole scene she stared at endless prairies, forests, lakes, rivers, and fields, all resonating with new life.

Then, at once, swirling around her and Justin, was the inner part of the rainbow of silver and gold. After taking a few whirls, it then burst into glittering threads. Julia watched how each thread dispersed, taking its rightful place among this new world. Right after it did so, Julia heard a man and a woman begin to laugh, a laugh of enjoyment, the kind you have with your very best of friends. Upon focusing her ears, the laugh was no longer just between two people but the jubilant laugh of a multitude.

At this, Julia heard a more powerful echo than before, the pronouncement of the words "very good."

The echo of these words hung like the last note of a concert symphony and then pleasantly faded away. This new world that she and Justin were in was more than just a place, it was a state of being, a masterpiece of art, and a vision come to life.

*   *   *

A cool breeze met Julia's face, gently rousing her from a tranquil rest as the rays of the golden sun poured through the trees.

Justin was already up and enjoying the surroundings. Over the fresh wind rode a cheerful merriment, which got closer and closer. Then in front of them were two people, a man and a woman. "Hello!" said the man. "I am Adam, and this is my wife, Eve."

Julia was about to respond, but then held back because there was now another person present too. It was one of the persons, the one dressed in garments of forest green and wearing a crown of emeralds. Julia again felt a presence of power, of beauty, and of might radiate from him.

Then, with a voice of love and joy, this person spoke to Adam and Eve and said, "My dearest children whom I have created in my image, I am God, the Father Almighty, Creator of the heavens and the earth. To you I give the gift of life, the gift of love, and the gift of this garden of Eden, which is the whole world. Be fertile and multiply and take dominion over this realm. All is yours, except for the tree of good and evil, which you are not to eat from, for if you do you will die. Rather, give attention on the Tree of Life, which I have placed at the center of this world as part of my gift to you."

Over the next several days, Julia and Justin, Adam and Eve, together with God himself, discovered what the garden of Eden was all about. The first thing Julia noticed was that there was an all-encompassing wonderful peacefulness. For the first time in a long time, she was without worry, stress, or angst. It was like a great weight had been lifted off her shoulders; she felt free, truly free. Oh, it was wonderful, and this alone would have been enough for her to want to stay in this garden forever!

Yet, as she continued to explore, she found that this was only the beginning of the garden's goodness. What else did she discover? She found that her needs and desires were all met, and neither she nor anyone else had to do any work. Yet, it wasn't a place of laziness; quite the opposite, she cared for the garden, its plants, and its animals. She and the others created; they were active. But their activity wasn't work. It was a joy. It was natural to her.

She also found that she, Justin, Adam, and Eve weren't just healthy in the general sense, but were the pinnacle of fitness and athleticism, beyond which could be found even in the best of

Olympians. She and Justin ran, swam, and never got tired. In fact, there was no such concept of sleep, and the term "rest" actually meant a form of appreciation and enjoyment.

Oh, but the nature itself! All of creation was in full concord. It was a masterpiece of thought, ideas, and diversity, all in synergy together. The splendor was not simply in that which Julia could detect with her five senses, it was also a majesty of honor, of virtue, and of purity.

She also found that she came to possess a special knowledge and wisdom. She could understand and appreciate what she was experiencing. She learned and her mind grew while there, but she was never in want of not knowing something that ought to have been known.

Yet, out of all the attributes she experienced, out of all the words she could use to describe it, the biggest reason Eden was Eden, and in which everything else flowed from, was that there was a complete harmony between her and neighbor, and between neighbor and God. Neither creation, nor humanity, nor God could be separated. God walked with her, Justin, Adam, and Eve each day throughout the garden, and they all were together in friendship as one.

After another day of exploration, Julia and Justin sat down under the shade of a large, leafy green tree. As a few bunnies stood at their feet, they discussed all that was going on.

As Julia reflected on the garden and her state of being, she found that it gave her a similar feeling to what she got when she remembered her best childhood memories. Except this was even better. This garden seemed to be the source of all the goodness that she ever felt in her life.

As Julia glanced down at the bunnies now asleep at her feet, she noticed a book entitled *Creation* laying on the grass. She picked it up and showed Justin who nodded. At that she opened the book and then found herself with Justin back in the forest library.

Chapter Three

ARROGANCE

FOR THE FIRST TIME in some time, Julia felt an idealism that seemed to have been bigger at some point, but lesser as of recent. It was like fanning an ember of a once-great fire, and for a brief moment a spring of hope welled within her.

She felt a longing and desire to bring such goodness to everyone else! Yet, even as she reflected on such optimism, she knew that such bliss was not the reality of her life or the world and that she had not a clue how to bring such goodness. It was like an impossible fairy tale—gorgeous but without a means to make it a reality.

Now the question upon her was thus: Why *isn't* the world perfect? Why isn't beauty and love all in all? What went wrong?

As she continued to consider such matters, Mary came into the library and joined Julia and Justin at the table.

"During your time in Eden," began Mary, "you experienced life as it ought to be, without any privation or deviance. The dream of making this vision a reality has been placed in the hearts of all humankind. It is the end to which all existence will eventually flow to by the might, love, and mercy of God. Eden is the vision that God has for the world and for all humanity. It is the North Star for anyone looking to do good."

The conversation then went on to where Mary set the stage for the next part of the journey. "To understand the need for redemption and salvation, it does one good to understand why that need came about in the first place."

Julia was mixed about this. She wanted to know; no, she *had* to know the answer. However, she was not delighted at the prospect. Her time in Eden had really made Eden hers. She didn't want to see something so beautiful decay.

After a period of silence, Mary gave a solemn nod, and at that, Julia went to pick a book on such a matter. It didn't take Julia long to find it, for on the same shelf as *Creation* she found the book entitled *The Fall of Humankind*. The cover was the scene of Eden but much faded and diminished.

She opened the book and again found herself and Justin back in the garden of Eden. However, this time she felt an eeriness and stillness which was not present the last time she was there.

"Doesn't seem quite the same, does it?" remarked Justin.

"No, it doesn't; I mean, of course it isn't," Julia replied as she looked around.

"There are Adam and Eve over there; it looks like they are talking to someone," pointed out Justin.

With that, she and Justin approached Adam and Eve to see what was going on. However, their greeting never happened. Before they finished walking to Adam and Eve, Julia stopped short and gave a shudder. For "standing" next to Eve was a horrific snake. It looked like a snake, but it felt to her more like a presence, like an entity, extremely cunning, very smart, and extremely powerful (although not all-powerful).

Julia saw that Eve and the snake were arguing as Adam stood nearby. No one took any notice whatsoever of her or Justin. Julia then listened to the conversation that seemed to already be in progress. In a confident and clear voice, the snake told Eve, "No, you did not pay attention. Did God really say, 'You shall not eat from any of the trees in the garden'?"

Eve paused, rolled her eyes, and then responded in an exasperated tone, "I have already told you, God said that we may eat of the fruit of all the trees in the garden; it is only about the fruit of the tree in the middle of the garden that God said, 'You shall not eat it or even touch it, or else you will die.' These were God's exact words, and I remember them specifically."

The snake gave a condescending look to Eve and said, "Die? You certainly will not die! No, when you eat of the tree you will be like gods, you will know good and evil, you will be true masters of this garden." In a sly and snobbish tone, the snake then started to bait Eve, "Do you just want to stay here and serve God? Or do you want to be your own master, to be a god yourself?

"Besides," continued the snake, "you will never be happy, knowing that you are lesser than God." Eve turned to the snake, and then to the tree with the forbidden fruit. Julia saw that Eve must have been having tremendous debate in her head. As Julia watched Eve look around at the rest of the garden, Julia felt as if all of creation was telling Eve not to listen to the snake, that what the snake was saying was just an empty lie. It was a lie because having been created in the image and likeness of God, Eve was as she ought to have been, she was not lacking anything, and her potential was boundless.

Julia wanted to run and tell Eve not to take the forbidden fruit, however, she felt as if her feet were glued to the ground. For a split second she watched Eve's eyes soften at the goodness of creation. For a moment Julia thought that maybe Eve would not take the forbidden fruit after all. However, this was a fleeting hope.

When Eve turned to look at the snake her eyes became fearful, disobedient, and envious, as if the snake were putting doubts and insecurities in her head. In the end, Eve took some of its fruit and ate it. Eve then handed the same fruit to Adam, who seemed to have had a similar debate in his mind that Eve had. However, like Eve, Adam took the forbidden fruit and ate it too.

Immediately after both Eve and Adam had eaten the forbidden fruit multiple things happened. A shadow fell, not only over the land and the skies but over the hearts and minds of all living things as well. It was a shadow that not only dimmed the light, but it was also a shadow of confusion, malice, disharmony, and anger. It was a shadow that lessened everything good of the world. But most of all, Julia perceived it as a shadow of *absence*.

As she stared at Adam and Eve she saw the looks of horror, of sadness, and even a hint of meanness in the eyes of both. Adam glared at Eve and Eve glared at the snake. The snake, however, seemed pleased with himself. Pleased with himself because now they were under his mastery of sin, of confinement, and of pride.

Then, with a mutual look of humiliation, Adam and Eve ran and hid from each other with both disappearing behind two different bushes next to where Justin and Julia were. A little while later they reappeared from the bushes, both wearing what looked like leaves hastily sewn together as clothes.

"This is an absolute disaster, how could—" but before Justin could finish speaking, he was interrupted by Julia who cut him off.

"Shhh . . . I think I hear footsteps."

"It's God," Julia heard Adam say in a frightened voice. "He usually comes to walk with us at this time of day," continued Adam. Adam paused and then suddenly whispered something to Eve. At that Adam and Eve again hid behind the nearest two bushes so as not to be seen.

Julia turned toward the direction of the footsteps, and there, right near her, stood God the Father in his green garments and crown of emeralds.

"Adam, Eve, where are you?" God asked as he looked towards the bushes that Adam and Eve were hiding behind. Then, like two children coming out of hiding to stand in front of a parent, Adam and Eve made their way and stood before God.

After an awkward pause, Adam answered in a timid voice, "Err, we were embarrassed because we were naked."

"Who told you that you were naked?" asked God.

And then it hit Julia, before the snake the term "nakedness" didn't exist in this garden, for before they were completely natural, comfortable, and respectable as they were.

Julia cringed at the conversation that ensued because it was not pleasant. God stood before Adam and Eve and questioned them if they had eaten from the forbidden tree.

God's voice had a tenor of discipline, of a controlled anger, a voice of a just parent about to confront their children about a terrible wrong they had committed. In answer to God's question, Adam honestly answered that yes, he did indeed eat from the forbidden tree. Then hastily, and with panic in his voice, he added, "But it was the woman you put here with me, she gave me the fruit to eat, it was her fault."

Julia winced, for she knew that was the wrong answer. By blaming Eve, his best friend, his wife, his soulmate, and not even calling her by her name, just made the mood that much more tense. Julia could feel God's disappointment. Justin simply scowled at the whole lot.

God then turned to Eve and asked, "What is this you have done?" Eve responded in the same timid voice that Adam had that it was the snake who tricked her into eating it. Clearly this was not a good answer either, but Julia thought that the look God gave to Eve was a bit softer than the one he gave Adam. Although, as Julia watched as God stared at Adam and Eve, Julia could tell that the guilt of the whole ordeal was equal between both Adam and Eve.

The snake was still present, and Julia thought it strange that the snake had stayed. But as God turned his gaze to the snake Julia gleaned a few things about it. By the look on the snake's face, she could tell that the snake actually had a better knowledge of who God was than Adam and Eve. That snake knew what he had done was wrong, knew he was going to be punished, and that there was nothing he could do about it. Hence, while giving God a look of hatred, the snake just stayed where he was.

God then spoke his sentences of penalty. Adam, Eve, and the snake were all to be punished. Yet, rather than being arbitrary, Julia saw the punishments were more a natural reaction to the events that had occurred. The snake's punishment was that it would now crawl on its belly and eat dirt.

For Adam and Eve, their punishments, that is, the natural effects of their sin, were as follows: hard labor would be required of the land to subsist, the bond of marriage would include difficulties, there would be pain in childbirth, and, worst of all, the fate of all living creatures would include death.

Then, both Adam and Eve, in tears of the realization of the wrong they had committed, were expelled from the garden of Eden. As they reached the edge of the garden (Julia had never noticed an edge before), Adam and Eve walked out of Eden. Julia and Justin had no choice but to follow them out. Behind them came a being (which Julia later found out to be a cherubim angel), with a fiery sword, who shut and locked the gate to the entrance of Eden.

As Julia and Justin stood just outside the gate of Eden and watched Adam and Eve walk away, Julia saw that with the fall of humankind a type of unwinding of creation occurred. Peace was interrupted by fear and worry, prosperity was no longer universal, that special health and fitness quality was lost, the beauty and harmony with nature was replaced by an arrogance and apathy towards creation, and the artful masterpiece of nature became faded and torn.

The synergy of diversity and culture which Eden was, was no longer so. The honor, purity, and innocence were gone. Knowledge and wisdom were lessened. But most of all, what made the fall of humankind so immoral was that the perfect harmony between God and Adam and Eve, and of all of creation among itself, was lost.

Julia's heart broke and she felt a flood of emotions. She felt sorry for Adam and Eve, but she also was angry at them. They had everything! Why did they have to eat from the forbidden tree? All they had to do was listen to God. If they did, everything would have remained as it ought to have.

Julia also felt cheated. She thought of what the world was and what her life would have been like if Adam and Eve were obedient as they should have been.

Julia and Justin simply stood there watching the figures of Adam and Eve get smaller and smaller in the distance. It was agony.

"I want to get out of here," said Justin with hurry.

"Me too," concurred Julia. She didn't have to wish for long. Next to her on a rock was the book entitled *The Fall of Humankind*. Upon opening it, Julia was no longer staring at a desert but at the shelves of the forest library.

Chapter Four

PEARLS OF LIGHT

As Justin sat with Julia in the forest library, he felt deflated. The main reasons for doubting the goodness of God occupied his mind. He longed for how he felt as he had in Eden proper, for while there he was free of whatever burdens he carried.

He had so many questions. Where *was* Eden? If the garden and the creation of the world was totally good, why was there a forbidden tree in the first place? And, how did the snake get into the garden?

Once Mary walked into the library, Justin voiced such concerns to her. Giving a knowing look, and with a voice of understanding, Mary said, "Come with me, I will show you."

She then went to the bookshelves where the book entitled *Creation* was. Yet, instead of picking out a book further to the right (which meant an event of a later date), she went and took one of many books to the left (which meant an event that far preceded *Creation*). Justin glanced at the book Mary now had in her hands. It was entitled *The Angels* and its cover was shiny and silvery.

Mary then opened the book, and at that Justin, with Julia and Mary, found himself on a dazzling snow-covered mountaintop. It was the height of daylight, and all was peaceful and quiet. From there could be seen a vastness of land, beautiful pine forests, and golden fields of hay dotted with amethyst flowers.

Beyond such features was more gorgeous forest which eventually gave way to plains of green grass. Far off, these plains ended at the edge of the river bright as glittering diamond. Beyond the river was an all-encompassing platinum light that shined with a brilliance of blessedness.

"Take a look to the west, and then let your eyes travel in a line going back from the forest library," said Mary. As Justin did so he saw a small clearing in the forest, and from that came a dancing light like that reflected off of emeralds, diamonds, and rubies. This light seemed to gently permeate the whole realm they were in.

"Is that where the three persons are?" asked Justin.

"Yes," replied Mary. Even from where he was, Justin could feel their special presence. As Justin watched the spot where they were, he saw a light emanate from them. It was similar to what he saw at the beginning of the creation of the world, that is, another rainbow of light, of thought, and of love.

This rainbow, instead of being different colors, was all shades of brilliant white, almost too bright to behold. As it reached the sky it became a starburst, and from it countless pearls of living light regally sparkled across the heavens.

As Justin observed these lights of force ballet in the heavens, he could feel their presence, and a new gladness stirred in his heart. In fact, as Justin stood watching this sight, one of these bright beings darted around him. As it did so, he felt a special connection to it, as if he and it were related in a special bond.

"Ah, the angels," said Mary as she gazed with a smile upon all that was unfolding. Turning to Justin and Julia, she explained, "What you are seeing is the creation of the angels, which were created by God far before your world began. God created them, like he does all things, out of his great love."

"Angels?" asked Julia with a quizzical expression. Mary smiled, opened the book she was still carrying entitled *The Angels*, and gave it to Justin and Julia to read, which went as follows:

At some "time" long before the world was created, out of his love, God created the angels to share in his glory, to live, and to love.

Angels are spiritual entities, what are called "immaterial" be-ings. Angels can and do travel through space and time at will, just like people travel in three-dimensional space. Even though angels have this flexibility, they are neither infinite nor eternal; those two attributes belong to God alone.

Angels, and humans for that matter, are what are called "ratio-nal beings," that is, they are beings of reason and logic. Even more fundamentally, a rational being is a being that makes the choice between good and evil. In fact, rational beings must make the choice between good and evil whether they desire to or not.

Angels and humans were designed by God to be a team. Angels are part of God's plan of salvation history. They bring messages (the term "angel" means "messenger"). Each human is paired with an angel in which that angel is that human's guardian.

For angels, as for humans, there is a tricky part about true love that must exist for it to be true, and that is that it must be freely chosen. Angels, like humans, need to choose love for it to be real. Because such a choice exists it means there are two options: to choose love or to refuse love.

At one point in "time," also before the creation of the world, the angels made their decision whether to choose love or not love, God or not God. Because of their special nature, angels make this choice once. It is not because they cannot change, but because they can travel across space and time, they have all the data when they make their choice (there would never be anything new to cause them to change). Hence, once they have chosen it is forever.

Two thirds of the angels chose love and became forever good and angels of God. However, due to the capital sin of pride, the other third of the angels rejected God, and went away from him. Because they went away from God, they, by their own hand, became demons, and became evil (evil is the absence of good). Where they live, since it is away from the light and love of God, is hell. Thus, evil existed before the creation of the world and so would have a tarnishing effect on anything created thereafter. The story of salvation and redemp-tion, that mission to which all are called, was already in progress before the time of the creation of the world.

As Justin finished reading, he had the feeling that he had already read such a book. Before he could ponder that question, a more relevant memory came into his head. He remembered his "ride" on the rainbow of thought that emanated from the three persons which lead to the creation of the world.

Justin remembered how when it first came from them it was pure, perfect, and pristine. As it traveled beyond and outward, however, he remembered how it passed through pockets of darkness which caused black threads to be intertwined in the rainbow. It was these black threads that had come to exist because of the fall of the angels, which allowed evil to become part of the world.

It was Julia who voiced Justin's conclusion when she opined, "Does this really mean that the world is still more good than not, and, that even though imperfect, humans are still in the image of God?"

Justin could tell, and was a bit surprised, that such an answer was especially important to Julia. As he saw the anguish in her face as she awaited Mary's answer, he became sure of it. He would make a point of gently asking more about this later.

After another moment, with soft eyes and a reassuring voice, Mary answered, "Yes, on both counts, just like you have always been taught since you were young."

In a more conversational tone, Mary continued, "To bring more illumination to the whole process of redemption, as you should remember from your journey thus far, God has already announced his plan to make things right, even before Adam and Eve left Eden. Yes, it is then when yours truly first enters the picture, a nice billing if I do say so myself."

Justin and Julia looked at each other. "I can't remember Mary being in Eden," whispered Justin to Julia.

"Neither do I," replied Julia. Justin looked at Mary with a puzzled expression.

"Alas, how did you miss me?" said Mary with a good-humored twinkle in her eyes.

After a period of silence Mary explained, "When God was giving the sentences of punishment to Adam, Eve, and the snake,

God also gave an announcement of hope. God said that a woman and her offspring were to do battle with the snake and that her offspring would win, meaning that good would triumph over evil."

Before Justin could dive into whatever that all meant, Mary spoke for his feelings, saying, "Yes, I know you have many questions on how this will happen and the who, what, and when. Like I have said, that is one of the reasons for this journey, and you will get all such answers in time."

Chapter Five

THE CHOICE

"Before the journey continues," said Mary after a time, "remember, up until now your journey has been beyond space and time, and dealing with realities presented in a way to teach and answer the question of 'why.' Going forward, your journey will now take place in real history, the same history written down in all the books one reads at university."

Mary then added, "As has already been said, whenever and wherever you go, you will fit in naturally, and those you interact with will know you appropriately. Everything will be in your understanding of colloquial English, dates used will be according to the system you know, and the like. Call it 'mysterious license,'" quipped Mary.

Julia laughed. "What?" said Justin, whose mind was still on the whole idea of living actual history.

"Mysterious license . . . like artistic license . . . get it?" retorted Julia. "How else could we simply stroll up and be part of the lives of the great figures and events of history without it being awkward?"

Mary then took on a more serious look and spoke. "As I have said, the rest of the journey will take place in real history, with real people, who have prayed real prayers. You both are an answer to some of their prayers. Just as you are being gifted with an answer to your prayers, you will indeed gift others with an answer to theirs. Many others are counting on you, more than you realize."

At that, Mary then handed them the book titled *God's Covenant*. Justin knew Mary had to have brought the book with her because they were still on the shining snow-covered mountaintop.

Mary explained, in a more teacherly tone rather than solemn, "You will now be going to the very nice estate of a husband and wife named Abram and Sarai in the town of Haran, a suburb of the great city of Ur in 1850 BC. Ur was one of the finest cities in the region. Located on the Euphrates River, it was the cultural center of its day. The city was home to large and decorative temples, government buildings, and multiple marketplaces. There were libraries, offices, and places to gather with friends. There were also schools with the flagship studies being math and astronomy. Ur was known for its suburbs and rich land used for farming and cattle grazing. The climate was well suited, and the Euphrates River was the source of irrigation."

Mary then went on to elucidate, "The only other information you need at present is that you are about to arrive on the day Abram and Sarai announce their decision to trust God and travel to the new land." She paused, and with a glint in her eyes added, "One more thing, just know that regardless of how it looks, Elam is indeed best friends with Abram and Sarai."

"Who is Elam?" asked Julia.

"You'll see," Mary responded with a smile. Mary then handed Justin the book entitled *God's Covenant*.

Justin studied the cover, which was a sketch of man with a smoking fire pot. He then opened the book. As they did so the whole scene changed. Justin found himself in a spacious room with large windows. The floor was covered with an ornate rug, and fine pieces of furniture were neatly placed throughout. In the center of the middle wall was a hearth which was home to a cozy fire.

As nothing was happening, Justin and Julia walked to the front of the fire and became immersed in its serenity. After some minutes, Justin was startled, for from behind them he heard, "Nice fire, I was about to start it up myself." Justin gave a small jump and quickly turned around. There, a few paces behind him, was a teenager that looked to be the same age as himself.

"Now that the fire is going let's head to the main dining room and see if there is any news on the rumors. The word is that Abram and Sarai are about to share some news that is going to drive my grandfather Elam crazy. So, this should be fun to watch," he said with a grin. "By the way my name is Sol." Justin and Julia then introduced themselves.

"Why is the news going to upset your grandfather?" asked Julia.

"Oh, it will be fine, they are all best friends, and my grandfather is the business manager of this estate. Apparently, Abram and Sarai have a plan that my grandfather thinks is completely ridiculous."

At that Justin and Julia followed Sol out the room into a hallway which opened to multiple rooms including those for living, cooking, and study. Justin walked past a decently wide staircase that led up to a second floor that seemed to have a similar architecture to the floor that they were on. The hall reached its destination at a large dining and entertaining room that was big enough to hold a large banquet.

Justin found it to be cool and comfortable. There were cushions, tables, and everything one would need to regularly host a large dinner party. It was half full of people, some eating, some discussing, some staring out the windows at the sunrise.

All of a sudden, Justin's ears were punctuated by the yelling of a man. "Did you get kicked by a donkey? Are you out of your mind?"

Justin turned to the source of the noise, which was from a man at the head of the table addressing a man and a woman who were next to him.

Justin saw Sol smile to himself as Sol said, "Here we go then. By the way, Elam is the one who just spoke and the man and the woman next to him at the head of the table are Abram and Sarai who are the estate owners," he whispered to Justin.

Justin then studied Abram and Sarai. He immediately was impressed by both of them. Abram seemed to naturally exude a sense of intelligence, kindness, and honor. Justin also found Sarai to project a similar vein, that is, one who was gentle, smart, and caring. He also guessed that all three of them, Abram, Sarai, and Elam, were in their mid-seventies.

Justin looked back at Elam who was glaring at Abram with a look of daggers. Elam then burst into it. "Abram, I humored you over drinks, I said 'yes' purely out of jest, I let this go on for a week, but now what do I see? I wake up, come down the stairs to my office, smell the fresh morning air and what is on my desk? A signed tablet by your hand selling this land to another property owner. The estate, the land, and the livestock. You *signed* this. Do you know what that means? Of course, you know what it means: it *means* that in a month we are out, done, gone!"

"Yes," replied Abram, "I know what a contract is, Elam, and, yes, we are going to prepare to go to the new land like we have already discussed."

Waving his hand, Elam continued as though without hearing Abram. "We have a choice piece of land; our profit has increased year over year for the past three years. We live in Ur, one of the best cities in the land. A city that has people who buy our grains and animals. It has doctors, it has libraries, it has, it has . . ." he stammered, "it has everything!"

Elam paused for only a second to catch his breath and went right back into it. "Not to mention that this is your father's house; you know that he is the one who acquired it all those decades back. This is our land, our ancestors lived here, this is our home!"

Elam seemed to be at the point of collapse out of pure exhaustion; his face was as red as the pomegranates on the table. Abram, with a conciliating smile, put his hand on his shoulder and spoke. "Old friend, we are called, and when we are called, we have to go." At that, Elam's eyes flickered only for a moment, but then he recovered his command and lit back into Abram, this time appealing to Sarai.

"Okay, fine, we move. And where are we going? All I can remember you telling me was that the land is far off. Where will we get employees? Will there be a market? What about a new house?

And . . . this new land, this new life . . . it is supposed to be better? So, I ask again, where is this new land anyway?"

"In the Negeb on the east edge of the Mediterranean Sea," replied Abram casually.

"In the Negeb . . . in the Negeb . . . you mean in the south of Canaan by the River Jordan? There is *nothing* there! Not to mention it already is peopled, the usual seminomads . . ."

Sol, with an audible giggle, said not so quietly under his breath, "Well, if it is peopled then the land clearly isn't wilderness." Some others giggled as well. It was enough to break the tension. Elam took a breath, and after a moment of silence, in more of a tone of pleading rather than anger, Elam implored, "The Negeb may be good land, yes . . . but . . . this land is better . . ."

By this time everyone who was in earshot had come into the room to see what all the fuss was about. Abram saw that those present were now looking to him for an explanation. He smiled and said, "Come gather around, I have news to share."

Abram paused and then explained, "About a month ago, I was out in the fields around sunset, it had just rained, and there was a nice cleanliness to the air. As I was gazing about the dusk I heard the voice of the Lord God—deep, rich, and wondrous—say to me, 'Go forth from your land, your relatives, and from your father's house to a land that I will show you. I will make of you a great nation, and I will bless you; I will make your name great, so that you will be a blessing. I will bless those who bless you and curse those who curse you. All the families of the earth will find blessing in you.'"

Abram stopped, and Justin could see a look of earnestness in his eyes. All present were silent. By the look on their faces, it could be seen that some were awed, that some doubted, and that most had many questions.

Abram continued, "How long have we talked about bringing faith into this world? How many times have we all prayed and yearned for a sense of purpose? How many times have we felt God tug at our hearts? We have been blessed, yet all of us have seen hardships. We have lost those we love; we have seen the poor and the sick in the streets; some we have been able to help, some not. We have seen the good and the bad, and, in our hearts, we know that the good is stronger.

"How will the good manifest itself? Such a question we have discussed many times. We now have an answer, and that answer is the Lord. A new era is dawning, and he is calling us to be part of it."

Abram, whom Justin found to be an elegant speaker, paused to let this sink in. He then went on, "Look, I do not know the future, and I do not claim to understand the mind of the Lord. I have asked myself the same questions you have all just murmured. While I do not have all the answers, I know that this is something we are called to do."

At that, Abram and Sarai left the room, as if to let what he had just said ruminate. The room then immediately erupted in chatter. Every inch of what Abram said was discussed, analyzed, and opinions freely given. Justin found the common opinion among the people, including Sol, was that while following God was agreed to be a good thing, there were many considerations. Was it indeed the Lord's voice that Abram heard? Why would the Lord ask them to leave all they had built? Is this in fact the purpose they have been looking for? These and more were the questions that Justin and Julia joined in to discuss.

After a couple of hours of conversations that showed no sign of slowing down, Justin nudged Julia so they could go outside to go for a walk, for he needed to think and converse just with her.

As they stepped outside, Justin found the picturesque view very pleasant. To the south were rolling fields of tall grass and hay. To the west and north were fields of bulls, cows, and chickens. At the edge of one of the fields was a row of small cottages. Even at this early hour there were already many people in the fields tending to the hay and the livestock. Justin could see why Elam was so upset; this was indeed a very enjoyable place.

As the days went by Justin and Julia became fast friends with Sol, who told them much about the lives of Abram, Sarai, and the whole estate. All in all, Justin saw that the question before Abram and his household was whether to trust in God or not. As he was feeling the same emotions as they were, he related to their trepidation, their desire for such a good thing to be true, as well as the fact that their future was unknown.

One day, a week since he and Julia had listened to Abram announce God's call, Justin was walking with Julia and literally stumbled across the book entitled *God's Covenant*. "Should we open it?" asked Justin to Julia.

Julia answered, "Depends. We can wait here until they go to the Negeb, I bet that will be very enlightening . . .

"Really though," she continued, "yes, it makes sense that we do, for most of what Sol told us clearly has more meaning for the future." So, Justin opened the book, clasped Julia's hand, and the whole scene changed.

He and Julia were now outside at nighttime. The moon, which was three quarters full, gave a silver white light that was enough to allow him to see the area. The land was grassy and mainly flat, with some small hills every now and then in the distance. There was a sense of openness and newness to the land.

As Justin looked to his left, he saw what could only be called a "tent village." In many of them he could see the yellow-orange light of lamplights. In front of some of the tents were also firelights burning from standing lamps.

As he continued to look about, Julia pointed and said, "Look, there is someone walking pretty quickly toward one of the larger tents." Justin looked to where Julia was pointing, and indeed, silhouetted against the moonlight was someone walking with an obvious sense of purpose.

"Let's see who they are," stated Justin. At that, he and Julia followed the person into the tent a minute or two after that person entered.

As he entered the tent, Justin's ears were greeted with the shouts of a man exclaiming, "Everyone, come over, yes, come in, something amazing just happened!" Justin turned to the man speaking and his mouth dropped open, for he was looking at none other than Abram himself. Abram was at least a decade older, but clearly still had the same energetic personality. There next to him was Sarai.

After less than a minute the tent was full of people, all with expectant looks to know what news Abram had to bring.

Abram raised his hands for silence so he could speak, and in a voice of excitement he began, "After my usual dinner walk, as the sun was starting to set with its golden rays upon me, I sat down outside on my favorite bench to take in the beauty of the evening. As I was sitting, I apparently fell asleep, because when I woke up it was already past twilight.

"I stood up to go back to my tent and then I stopped in my tracks, for there in front of me, out of nowhere, appeared a medium-sized smoking pot filled with fire and a torch with yellow and orange flames. On both sides of the flaming pot were the halves of animals. Then I watched as the torch and smoking pot moved and passed between those halves of animals.

"As this was happening, I heard the deep and fatherly voice of the Lord, who said to me, 'Abram my dear child, this new land that you are in, as well as its surrounding land, is given to your descendants.'

"After God's message finished, the pot of flames and smoke, the torch, and the animal offerings disappeared. I then woke up and discovered that what I just saw was a vision from God the Lord!"

Abram paused with a smile on his face. "I surely need some more context for this," whispered Julia to Justin.

"Let's see if he explains further," he answered. Justin and Julia did get a further explanation, but it was not from Abram but from Elam. Elam, with the same self-assured and animated personality, went on to explain to all those in the room that what Abram just witnessed was the official process of signing not just a contract but a treaty, as in a treaty between major tribes and even states. The signatories of such treaties were the heads of state themselves.

How this worked was that animals were ceremoniously cut up to signify what would happen to a party if they ever broke the treaty. The flaming torch and smoking pot represented the signature, which in this case was the signature of God. Elam couldn't seem to impress upon them how meaningful this was. Elam squarely ended by saying, "Yes, the Lord is absolutely going to give you such descendants and land as he has told you he would."

"Ah, good ole Elam," said Julia to Justin with a laugh. "He hasn't changed one bit!"

As Justin and Julia stepped back outside together, Julia said, "So, that whole covenant thing Abram was talking about must be true. And, this place must be the Negeb." This seemed a good-enough explanation to Justin, that is until he had a realization that seemed to have poured cold water on the cheery atmosphere. For then he just remembered how Sol had explained to them that Abram and Sarai could not have children.

Sol had explained it in detail. Abram and Sarai had seen many doctors and tried all that they could, but it was never to any avail. In fact, the hope of them having children was already deemed closed years ago.

If that wasn't enough to burst Justin's bubble, Abram and Sarai were now even that much older, and Justin did not need to be a doctor to know perfectly well that there was no way Abram and Sarai could have any descendants.

"Kids, Julia, they cannot have kids!" Justin stammered.

He looked at Julia, who replied, "Well, this makes no sense then. How can God make a covenant with someone's descendants if they can't have any? Let's go find that book so we can go back to the forest library and ask Mary."

"Agreed," said Justin. So, he and Julia went searching for the book entitled *God's Covenant*. Finding it on a nearby bench, Justin picked it up and opened it. The scene changed, but not as Justin expected it to. Instead of being back in the forest library, he found himself still in the same complex of tents. He stood not under moonlight but in the light of an early dusk.

Chapter Six

AN ACT OF COURAGE

SEEING THAT, NOW, THERE was a large tent next to them, Justin said, "Well it's not the library, but still, let's go check out this tent; maybe we can find some answers." As he and Julia walked into the tent, Justin found the tent had only a single occupant, which was Sarai sitting peacefully doing some knitting. Much time must have passed again, for Sarai looked to be at least another decade older.

Just as Sarai was turning her head to look at who walked into the tent, suddenly the peace and quiet was interrupted by Abram who rushed inside and exclaimed, "Sarah! Sarah! God did it! God did it! Our prayers have been answered!" Talking a million miles a minute, Abram hugged Sarai and leapt about.

"What prayers? What happened? Calm down, I can't even understand what you are saying . . . why are you calling me 'Sarah?' Have you been having a couple of drinks?" cried Sarai wide-eyed.

"Sit down, wait, let me get the rest of the family. Elam!" yelled Abram.

A moment later Elam, along with some others, appeared, and Sarai commanded, "Okay Abram, out with it already!"

"I was out on my usual after-dinner walk, and suddenly, the Lord appeared to me quite unexpectedly. God reiterated the covenant between us and our descendants—you know, the one with the torch and smoking pot from all those years ago—and then God said, 'Your wife Sarah is to bear you a son, and you shall call him 'Isaac.' It is with him that I will maintain my covenant as an everlasting covenant and with his descendants after him.'

"We are having a boy, Sarah, you and I, and, it is through him that the covenant will be fulfilled!"

Sarai leapt up and hugged Abram, and she became just as giddy as he was. The whole room instantly became alive with joy. After many hugs, kisses, and handshakes, everyone settled down. It began to sink into Justin that what was happening was nothing short of a miracle. He could clearly see both Abram and Sarai were in their nineties. He also could see their sturdy faith, that they truly believed that God could do the impossible, and that they were completely confident they were going to be parents.

Elam then chimed in, "Why do you keep calling Sarai 'Sarah'?" Abraham then explained that since the covenant was to be everlasting the Lord changed their names: Abram to Abraham and Sarai to Sarah. For the name "Abraham" means "father of a multitude of nations" and the name "Sarah" means "princess."

After Abraham finished explaining, Elam gave a whistle and said, "I always knew we had royalty in the family!"

Justin and Julia couldn't help but rejoice with the rest of the family at this truly miraculous news. Then a person next to them said, "Amazing, isn't it?" Justin turned to find that Mary was standing next to them. She, too, was displaying the joy of the evening. The three of them then went outside and leisurely strolled the grounds as the last vestiges of blue and purple light fell upon the grassy plain.

As they walked, Mary revealed that, indeed, within a year's time Abraham and Sarah would give birth to a beautiful baby boy and name him Isaac, who would grow up to be one of the patriarchs of old.

Mary also described that three promises were given in this covenant: the making of Abraham and Sarah a father and mother of great nations and leaders; blessing them and their descendants; and giving them the land of Canaan (of which the Negeb is a part).

Justin marveled at all he had witnessed and what Mary had just explained. A miracle baby, a promise of God, and the dawn of a new age. As he was thinking he asked aloud, "Abram . . . I mean Abraham . . . was seventy-five years old back in Haran. Now he must be in his nineties . . ."

"Ninety-nine to be exact," clarified Mary.

"Okay, ninety-nine. So what happened during the past twenty-five years?"

"Also," added Julia before Mary could respond, "now that I think about it, when I looked around, I saw other people who looked almost like kings and queens, and that the tent was very nicely furnished with art, decorations, and jewelry that were even fancier than anything I had seen back at Abraham's estate in Haran. I mean, if they are in the wilderness, how do they know all these very important people and where did they get the art from?"

"And," voiced Justin, "these two times when Abraham talked about the power of God, everyone seemed to take it as fact right away, like they all knew God, whereas before in Haran God was a big debate."

Mary smiled with a look of admiration at the two of them and answered, "Indeed, a lot went on in the past twenty-five years."

Mary then continued, "It was these twenty-five years that set the stage for the rest of the salvation history. These years were full of fascinating events: a temporary move to Egypt due to a famine, then followed by resettlement at the Negeb; the making of a name for Abraham and Sarah's household by helping to drive out other nations of aggressors in the War of the Kings, and by the gaining of wealth and property. There was even a visit by a most fascinating figure by the name of Melchizedek."

Justin pondered all of this as they continued their stroll around the grounds. The last bit of twilight had given way to a blanket of red, blue, white, and gold stars. He had never seen such a night sky of stars so bright or so many. Such a scene reinforced the line from God that Abraham and Sarah's descendants would be as numerous as the stars. With this he felt a spiritual wonder at it all.

"Now, we'll visit Abraham's seventeen-year-old son Isaac, the miracle baby's announcement that we just celebrated. Here we'll witness God give a message in a most unforgettable way."

At that, Justin, with Julia and Mary at his side, found himself on a mountainside. The incline was gradual, with trees and bushes all around. Then, not too far in front of where he was standing, Justin saw a teenager that he knew had to be Isaac.

Isaac had brown hair, was strong, and had a look in his eyes of a wisdom beyond his years. With Isaac was Abraham, as well as two attendants and a donkey, who were carrying the wood for a fire.

As Justin got closer to them, he was able to see their expressions. Abraham's mood was clearly one of anguish and looked as if he was having a terrible debate in his head. Isaac, on the other hand, seemed relaxed and to be enjoying the scenery of the hike.

As they followed them up the mountain Mary took the time to explain the background to this all in detail. What happened the day prior was this. Abraham was preparing dinner when suddenly the Lord called out to him. Abraham, who was happy to hear the Lord's voice, called back, "I am here." However, as soon as the Lord spoke Abraham lost all eagerness. What the Lord said to him was that he called on Abraham to sacrifice Isaac as a burnt offering to him. The Lord told Abraham to go to Mt. Moriah early the next morning and do so. That was all the Lord said and there was no further explanation.

Suffice it to say Abraham did not sleep that night. He pondered and pondered. It was nearly forty years since God had first called him from his old land in Ur to resettle in the Negeb. In the time since, God had blessed him with land, a son (who was literally a miracle), and much prestige. The covenant that God made was indeed manifesting itself. Abraham and his family were not just prospering temporally but spiritually. They helped others, and people came to them for prayers and for spiritual advice. Angels had even visited him.

It was in this background that Abraham agonized over the command God had just given him. It did not make sense. To sacrifice one's son, his son whom he loved, was untenable! As he deliberated, he saw that the question at hand was not whether to sacrifice Isaac, but whether to be obedient and to trust in God.

To Abraham, the answer to that question was clearly "Yes." Abraham knew that to be obedient and trusting was the right attitude before God. Even so, not for a moment did it ever slip Abraham's mind that this meant sacrificing Isaac. Abraham was also determined to give the final choice to Isaac. For Isaac also had a deep friendship and faith with God.

In summation, Abraham knew that the right and just decision was to follow God's command, not just for him, but for Isaac too. If Abraham didn't have the relationship with God that he did, if they had not become the true friends that they were, if he did not lead the life of faith that he did, if Abraham didn't let God pour into his heart and mind day after day after day, he never could have come to such a decision. In the end it was obedience and trust. This is what God was calling Abraham to.

After Mary finished giving Justin and Julia this background information, Justin halted. He could not believe Mary. What kind of God would ask someone to sacrifice their own son? Yes, he understood the honor of giving one's life for another in an extraordinary circumstance. But here, as he watched Isaac in all his youth and idealism walk side by side with Abraham, such a command seemed pure madness.

Julia then questioned, "God asked Abraham to kill Isaac, his miracle son. Why? What good would that do?"

By now all three of them were stopped, and Mary turned to them, and in a tone of more gravity they had yet seen her have, spoke to them. "Evil and sin, as you have seen, entered the world through pride, the sin that is the antithesis of the very nature of God. Likewise, the worst effect of sin and evil is death. If you look back at all that was lost at the fall of the angels and the fall of the garden of Eden, all losses have their point of origin in pride and death."

Mary gave a moment of silence and then went on: "Therefore, the only remedy for pride and death is their opposites, love and life. It is through the ultimate act of love and life that your world will be glorified, yet not only your world but all of existence itself."

After a time, Abraham, Isaac, and the others they were with came to a stop. Justin then watched them build a simple altar with stones, and upon it they laid the wood logs for burning on the top of it. It was here that Justin noticed a curious look on Isaac's face. Still standing a small distance away, Justin, Julia, and Mary observed what unfolded next.

Abraham turned to Isaac, put his hand on his shoulder, and then spoke to him. Their voices were low, and Justin could not hear what was said, but he could guess. Isaac's face became grave, and Abraham's eyes became misty. After a time, they then embraced. To Justin's great surprise, he saw Isaac climb upon the altar of his own accord with a face of resoluteness and courage.

It is hard to describe what happened next. Abraham pulled out a long metal knife, raised it over the body of Isaac, and prepared to strike. It was a terribly strange scene. As Justin stared, he saw that Abraham meant to go through with it and was going to strike.

Then, at the very last second, a deep and powerful voice emanated from the sky: "Abraham! Abraham!" It was so powerful and so commanding that everyone froze in their positions.

Abraham, upon hearing the voice, shouted, "Here I am! I am here!"

The voice, which was that of an angel, continued, "Do not lay your hand on the boy. Do not do the least thing to him. For now, I know that you fear God, since you did not withhold from God your son, your only one."

At this, Abraham threw the knife to the ground and Isaac jumped off the altar. Surreally, they stood in the utmost relief.

Several minutes later, Abraham heard a rustle and saw a ram whose horns had been caught in a thicket next to them. Together, Abraham and Isaac offered this ram as the burnt offering in place of Isaac.

As Justin observed the ram being sacrificed instead of Isaac, an understanding washed over him. He came to understand what it meant to have faith and trust, and what it meant to be obedient. Abraham and Isaac were not obedient and trusting because of book learning or blind belief. They did so out of love, out of friendship, out of embracing the mystery of faith.

He also laughed at himself for getting so tense. Of course, God wasn't going to have Abraham kill his own son! It was all part of the grand design of God. How could it not be? As he looked upon Abraham and Isaac arm in arm smiling together, he no longer saw a man and a teenage son, but two great patriarchs of old.

Justin's gaze upon them was then broken by another voice from heaven. It was still just as powerful as the first, but this one was more joyful and victorious. It was the angel again, who directed his message to Abraham: "The Lord pronounces that because you acted as you did in not withholding from me your son, your only one, I will bless you and make your descendants as countless as the stars of the sky and the sands of the seashore; your descendants will take possession of the gates of their enemies, and in your descendants all the nations of the earth will find blessing, because you obeyed my command."

Justin and Julia watched Abraham and Isaac walk away with joy continuing to radiate from them both.

Justin, Julia, and Mary then leisurely walked down through the woods of the mountain. "What you have just witnessed," began Mary, "was the seventh and final communication and action regarding the Abrahamic covenant, or better said, the beginning of the great covenant between God and the descendants of Abraham and Sarah. Now, the process of events that are to bring redemption from God to his people, including you two, are now in progress."

Mary then made the point that the fall of humankind was now in the process of being reversed. She explained how at the fall of Eden, the first thing to break was the relationship between God and humans and humans with each other. With the covenant of Abraham and Sarah in progress, that relationship was restarted between humankind and God, and humankind and each other.

As Justin took in Mary's words, and as he considered everything he had experienced concerning Abraham, he could see that something wholly new had begun, something that would lead to something even bigger. It was like seeing a sprout of great oak arise from the ground.

As they continued their pleasant stroll about the mountainside, Julia asked, "So, what is next?"

Mary then took out two books she had brought with her, one entitled *Midian*, which she handed to Justin. The other was entitled *Goshen*, which she handed to Julia. Mary then said, "So far, you have experienced the creation of the angels, the creation of your world, and the sprouting of God's plan to bring about salvation and redemption. From now on, you will be an essential part of salvation history itself."

Chapter Seven

PERSISTENCE

"THIS CAN'T BE RIGHT," assumed Julia as her eyes adjusted to the darkness she was in. Well, it was not fully dark; there was a trivial light from a small lamp. To her dismay she discovered that she was in a cramped room with five other people.

All five of them were covered in dirt, were sweaty, and carried a look of resignation. They included a girl who looked the same age as her, and even though this girl was covered in dust Julia could tell she was very pretty. There was also a boy a few years younger, a man and a woman who Julia guessed were the parents, and an elderly lady who certainly fit the bill of a grandmother.

There was no conversation, and it all looked like they had just finished getting ready to turn in for the night. "Night Julia," said the girl next to her. At that, the whole family seemed to fall asleep in an instant. Julia, who was wide awake with confusion, took this chance to walk around this "house" she was in.

She quickly discovered that it wasn't a house and that her walk around the abode lasted only thirty seconds. Rather than an actual house, it was a large single room with a few alcoves being the only attribute that gave the place a sense of having different areas. There was a fireplace, but it was old and crumbling. The main area was covered with mats for sleeping and chairs dotted the perimeter. She could tell that in the daytime the chairs and sleeping mats would be positioned in reverse. The walls were plain, dusty, and the tables were absent of any useful tool.

After this dismal tour of the place, Julia thought about going outside to see what it was like. However, something told her it would be best to wait until morning. As she took another look around, she thought again how this didn't seem right at all. She had just "left" the pinnacle of Abraham, Sarah, and Isaac; thus, she thought things should be much better than what she was seeing.

Not liking the situation at all, she then searched around for the book entitled *Goshen*, the one that had brought her here, but it was nowhere to be seen.

"'Goshen.' What does that mean?" she thought to herself. After doing another search for the book, which was again futile, she did the only thing she could do: lay back down on the sleeping mat and eventually fell into an uneasy sleep.

Julia was awakened by the clanking of metal pots and utensils. The rest of the family was already up. The door to the place was open and Julia could see the dark blue-gray light of an early dawn. Then, the girl who said "good night" to her yesterday seized Julia's wrist and while lifting her to her feet said in a hurry, "I know yesterday was worse than normal so we let you sleep, but now we really must go. I don't want to deal with their nonsense two days in a row. Let's just go, do our work, be invisible, and get back here."

Given the tenor of the girl's voice, Julia obeyed. As they were walking out the doorway, Julia heard the woman say, "Hannah, don't forget your water canteen, and be sure Jehu gets an easier job today like throwing in straw." Jehu, apparently Hannah's younger brother, then joined them in the doorway. Julia could tell no one was happy.

Out of instinct, Julia looked at the grandmother who replied with a caring voice, "Just keep your heads down; the workday will be done before you know it."

"Yes, remember those wise words from Lena," replied the man, Hannah's father, who himself gave a small smile, clearly trying to give some encouragement.

Bewildered, Julia followed Hannah and Jehu out the doorway. She found herself outside in what she could see was a poor section of a crowded town. On each side of a dusty dirt road were rows of tenements in disrepair. Out of them came people of all ages who were walking in the same direction as she was.

No one was content or really awake. The only auditory thing she heard was a few grumbles from some of the people around her. She continued to follow Hannah and Jehu, first out of the rows of tenements to a more open space, and then as the sun rose, they walked down a slightly sloping plain that, not too far in the distance, terminated into a large and slow-moving river. Beyond that, she saw a large city; even from this distance she could tell it was grand. As they kept walking, they came to a place dotted with pits of reddish-brown mud and piles of yellow straw.

Julia was astonished by the number of people there. She also came to the realization that there were clearly two classes of people. A class like herself and Hannah's family, who wore old clothes and lived in the tenements. The other class was clothed in nice white cloaks with jewelry of gold, or was wearing bronze armor with fancy insignia.

Up until now, Julia had tried to stay in denial of the reality that she had found herself in. However, any hope of that was completely dashed with what occurred next. For she was shocked to see Hannah, as well as those around her, take off their sandals and get into one of those pits and begin to mix up the mud while some others, including Jehu, threw straw in.

Julia stood in disbelief. Yet she did not stand idle for long, for one of the men wearing armor yelled at her to get to work while pushing her into the pit. Headfirst she fell into a yucky goo of mud and crushed straw. After wiping her eyes as best she could she saw Hannah glaring at the man who threw Julia in.

"It's okay," comforted Hannah to Julia as she helped her back up. "Just make bricks and think of that cool well water we can wash off with tonight after work."

As nice as fresh cool water is, such a thought was not enough to ease her or take away the dread that had now filled her. As time went on the day seemed to never end, and she was never allowed to rest. By the time she, Hannah, and Jehu were finally released to go home, Julia was sore, tired, and thirsty.

To her dismay, she, Hannah, and Jehu repeated this day's events the next day, and the next week, and the next month. Julia could sum up this part of the journey in a single sentence: wake up, make bricks, wait for something bad to happen, come home, go to sleep, and then repeat.

Each day, Julia had kept her eyes open for that stupid book so she could get out of there. However, to her consternation, it never appeared.

She did, however, thanks to many talks with Hannah and her grandmother Lena, come to find out the answers to exactly when, where, and who she was with. The first thing she came to find out was that the descendants of Abraham and Sarah called themselves the "Israelites." As to where and when, the answer was Goshen, the Israelite village in Egypt, in the year 1250 BC. She was with an Israelite family who was just like any other. The Israelites had been in slavery for over a century.

In terms of Lena, her story was not that of someone who had a wonderful life that was lost because everything fell apart. No, it was nothing that dramatic. She was seventy-one, and what she did at present, she did when she was five, at seventeen, at fifty-nine, all the way up to today. Eight years ago, her husband collapsed while working under the bitter, hot sun. Those with him tried to help but it was no use. He died while mumbling a prayer that was inaudible. As for Hannah, no more excitement could be said of her life than for Lena.

Life was terrible for the Israelites, but Julia came to very much admire them, for she saw them as a model of realistic courage. They had a faith that seemed always to be tested but was never wholly broken. Even though they didn't have much hope, they did not despair. What struck Julia most about the Israelite community was their heart and their culture. They cared about and for each other. They had elders. They had traditions. They had faith—faith in their God, the God of Abraham.

As to how the current circumstances came about, this is what happened. Abraham's son Isaac grew up and married a girl named Rebekah. They had multiple sons, one of them being Jacob who grew up and followed the Lord in an extra-special way. At the Lord's bidding, Jacob's name was changed to Israel, for he was to be the father of the twelve tribes. This is why they call themselves "Israelites." Jacob was married twice, and in total had twelve sons. One of those sons whom he had with his wife Leah was named Judah.

In the 1700s BC, due to a famine, the whole Israelite people moved into Egypt. The eleventh son of Jacob, Joseph, became a high leader of Egypt and the Israelite people were warmly welcomed. For over two centuries the Israelite people flourished, life was good, and it was an era of happy memories.

As time went on, however, the prestige of Joseph and the benevolence of the Egyptian leaders of old were forgotten. The new Egyptian leaders became afraid of the Israelites for they were jealous of their number, wisdom, and prosperity. Slowly but surely the Israelite people became increasingly marginalized. They first lost their prestige, then some basic rights, then their money and their property. Then they became something that resembled indentured servants.

By the 1300s BC their position had fallen to its low point. They were now slaves of the Egyptians and were in bondage with no rights whatsoever. Life was miserable, hard, and unfair. The Egyptians had all the advantages—not just in the military or taskmaster's with whips, but that they had control of every inch of the Israelites. If the Egyptians wanted to take away their food and water they could; if they wanted to split up friends and families they could.

It was in this chain of events that Julia found herself to be living. Whatever was going to happen in the future was completely and utterly out of their hands. It was only God that could rescue them.

Julia was honestly disappointed. She had left Isaac with great hope, but now it seemed that everything had fallen apart. She kept asking herself how in the world could something like this be part of God's plan, especially a plan that was supposed to make things better?

Another day had gone by. It was late at night, and before bed the whole family, including Julia, would pray to God for deliverance. Each night a different person would lead. Sometimes it would be earnest, sometimes simply recited without caring, but they always did it. That night after their prayer, Jehu looked up to Hannah and said, "Maybe God will rescue us soon."

Hannah smiled back, said "Maybe," and then went to sleep.

The next day, Julia and Hannah came back from the brick pits with their feet as sore as ever. When they got back, Julia found that most people were outside and everyone was talking at the same time; some of the louder ones were sayings things like:

"Who is Moses?"

"Moses came back?"

"You mean the Prince of Egypt?"

"That was decades ago, who cares?"

"Did he really talk to God?"

However, there were so many people excitedly talking at once that Julia could not get a clear representation of what was going on. Finally, she and Hannah found a speaker who Hannah recognized as one of the elders.

"Let me repeat, hold on, quiet," directed the elder. "I am talking about the Moses of the story we have been retelling for all these years, that he has come back to Egypt." The speaker paused. "Not only that, but in his time away he spoke with God himself." At that the people in the circle gasped. The speaker put up his hands to silence his listeners.

"In the coming days, Moses and the elders will go to Pharaoh to tell them that our God, the God of Abraham, commands him to let us go free. Not only this, but God has given Moses a special power to convince Pharaoh." All were silent. The speaker then went on. "This is all I know and all I have heard. Let us pray and hope." At this the speaker left to presumably go share the same news with others.

Julia and Hannah just stared at each other for a moment. "Could this really be true?" Hannah asked Julia. Julia was intrigued. It's one thing for God to lead a band of people from Mesopotamia to the Negeb. It was another to free people from the most powerful and advanced nation-state in the region. This was going to be a colossal endeavor.

"I hope so," Julia answered.

"Yes, I do think so," Hannah replied as she gave a small smile back. They then both joined the many conversations that were going on around them.

The next few days saw a change in the attitude of the Israelite community. While news effectively spread, Julia, Hannah, and the family did not get to see Moses or the elders. Goshen was large and traveling across it from where they were took time and energy, neither of which anyone had. So, while a good number of people were able to see or hear Moses give reports from time to time, the majority did not.

Julia and Hannah heard the next piece of news on an evening. The expected first meeting between Moses and Pharaoh took place earlier that day and all were awaiting the results. Julia could feel the excitement in the air, for there was a genuine thought that their release could take place within days.

The crescendo of excitement that built during the day, however, quickly evaporated when actual news came. The meeting between Moses and Pharaoh did not go well. Not only was it a failure, but it made matters worse. To make the point that he was all-powerful, Pharaoh ordered that the Israelites now had to find their own straw to make bricks while keeping their quotas. After listening to such reports, all returned to their homes in angst.

"That is impossible!" Hannah yelled furiously to the rest of her household. "Now what is going to happen?" No one responded to her because they all felt the same way. It was bad enough to have the rescue be a failure. It was even worse to lose the straw for the bricks.

As the days went by, Julia found that life became even worse than it was before. Sleep seemed nonexistent and the hope of

Moses appeared dashed. To add insult to injury, the Egyptians at the brick pits now mocked the Israelites, saying that all Moses' presence would do is make things worse.

When the residents of Goshen heard that Moses was going to speak to Pharaoh again, they were not happy. In fact, some pleaded that he not. Why make matters worse? Julia thought it was a fair question.

On the day of the second scheduled meeting between Pharaoh and Moses, all the talk at the brick pits was speculation about what would come of it. Some held out hope, but most had decided they would be happy if the status quo was not made worse. Julia was resigned and did not get involved in the debate. She just wanted to get the bricks done before dark so she could sleep for a decent amount of time.

After an hour of straight work, Julia, in deciding to give herself a break, took a moment and looked out at her surroundings. To her surprise everyone else seemed to have taken a pause too. Julia nudged Hannah who was next to her and saw that everyone had gotten out of the brick pits and was looking in the same direction.

As she turned her head to look in the same direction her jaw dropped. As she and Hannah stared at the Nile River, Julia did not see a wide, meandering, sparkling river, but a river that was red, blood red, like a long open gash upon the land.

"That is impossible! I was just down there getting water less than fifteen minutes ago," stammered one of the Egyptian guards in a frantic voice. "The water was as clean as normal!"

The other guards looked at him for some explanation. He continued in disbelief as he pointed toward a nearby container. "I'll show you. I filled this vessel of water myself from the Nile less than a quarter of an hour ago." However, when he looked inside the container, he let out a piercing scream of fright. As he jumped back from it, he knocked it over. As it and its contents fell to the ground what was seen was not fresh water, but blood which spilled onto the ground for everyone to view.

There were gasps and yells of shock. One of the taskmasters started yelling at the Israelites to get back to work. However, no one listened, and even he seemed to be doing it only as a reflex action. Julia didn't know how to react, for she was just as frightened as the others. "The water turning to blood? This is bad, very bad," said Hannah in a voice of terror. "Let's get out of here and go back to Goshen!" Hannah demanded frantically. With that Hannah and Julia left the brick pits as fast as they could. No one stopped them.

When Julia and Hannah got back to Goshen, Hannah immediately ran to one of the wells because she was worried that it may now contain blood too. She threw in a bucket and pulled it up as fast as she could as Julia watched at her side. Once she got it up, she hesitated for a moment. Then she slowly peered into it ready to throw it away. Instead of tossing it, Hannah gave a sigh of relief. What was in her bucket was clear, cool, regular well water.

"It's all right," came a calming voice. Lena approached them and gave them each a comforting pat on the shoulder. "Come, let's walk and I'll explain as best as I can."

Before Lena began to speak, Hannah asked all at once, "Did God actually turn the water into blood? What does that even mean? Is Pharaoh going to let us go now?"

Lena gave a look of seriousness and replied, "We will indeed go free, but not yet." Julia had found that Lena, while she was not an elder herself, had many friends, was well liked, and had many sources of accurate information.

Lena went on, "It will take some time. God is going to work wonders to free us, the first of which you have seen today. These wonders will show that our God, the God of Abraham, is indeed *the* God."

Lena then explained the story of the covenant of Abraham and how whatever was happening now is its next part. She also stressed that their rescue would take time and not all of it would be easily understood.

"How anyone can ignore the fact that the River Nile is now blood," finished Lena, "I cannot begin to speculate. That should be enough to convince anyone! Alas, it will take more time and wonders to convince Pharaoh. Never underestimate the errors that pride and arrogance bring."

Over the next several weeks, Julia saw and heard signs and wonders that she never thought she would observe. There were plagues of frogs, flies, and disease. Each halted the day-to-day life of the Egyptians and caused much distress. Even so, as Lena had predicted, Pharaoh would not let the Israelites go.

Yet, even though they were not yet free, progress could be seen. Events such as these, even if not recognized by all, still cause major changes. While Pharaoh and his associated leaders stayed stubborn and set a strong face, after a while, much of the Egyptian government had neither the will nor the stupidity to do the same. Workers stayed home, fear was high, and portions of the government ceased to function.

While Julia, Hannah, and the rest of the Israelites were still forced to work, the intensity was no longer what it once was. There were no longer whippings, yelling, or long hours. The Egyptian taskmasters, supervisors, and architects had taken note of these plagues as they had caused direct angst to their lives and their families. Many Egyptians were out of commission because they were still recovering from being sick. They were also thirsty, hungry, and sleep deprived from not being able to rest due to the frogs.

However, Julia, Hannah, and the rest of the Israelites had a much better fare because where they lived and worked were free of the plagues. There were not any frogs, disease, or other detrimental effects. Whether they were in Goshen or at their worksites, harm did not befall them. The Egyptians quickly figured this out and spent as much time as they could at the Israelite worksites. Julia found this swing in power most welcome.

As Julia and Hannah were sitting by one of the wells in Goshen, Hannah turned and asked, "Julia, do you know what I am doing right now?"

Julia looked back at Hannah and replied, "Ummm . . . nothing?"

"Exactly!" she shouted back with glee. "I'm really glad you're here, Julia. You mean a lot to me. I don't know if I could have gone through all of this without you."

Julia was very moved by such a compliment. Indeed, she felt connected with her, not just in their friendship, but it was as if she had known Hannah for years. Walking side by side with her in need and trying to be of help and support was strangely familiar. Yes, she felt as if she had done this before.

"Hey, I feel the—"

Before Julia could continue her thoughts, Hannah interrupted her; this time her voice was not one of glee but one of surprise. "Stop! Look at that. Look at what is right over the Egyptian city!"

Turning, Julia saw what Hannah was seeing. "Whoa . . ." responded Julia with the same emotion as Hannah.

Julia saw the oddest site she had ever seen. Here in Goshen the sun was shining upon her with blue sky overhead. But over the Egyptian city were menacing, dark black clouds. From these clouds rained hail and lightning more severe than she had ever seen. Even from her position she could see fires erupt from where the lightning strikes hit. Such a spectacle went on for hours, over the city, over the palace, and over the Egyptians' fields and livestock. All the while, not even a single wisp of a cloud disturbed the sun that shown upon Goshen.

"That has to be it, no one can go on after that!" Hannah declared to Julia later that evening once the storm was over. Hannah was indeed correct, because when they arrived at the brick pits the next day, Julia saw that things were no longer the same. In fact, Julia came to find that the entire system had broken down. The hailstorm was indeed the turning point. From this day forth, neither Julia's nor Hannah's feet would ever again step in a brick pit, nor their hands cut straw, nor their efforts do anything for Egypt.

It was also around this time that Julia voiced the observation that there was something else peculiar going on. Ever since Moses came back, she had noticed the general populace of Egyptians becoming a lot more friendly towards the Israelites. What was most surprising was that it seemed genuine.

In fact, many Egyptians were even donating gold, silver, and clothes to the Israelites for their new life. Friendship was one thing, but giving up money was another. So, Julia was utterly stunned that this was going on. Julia, while elated at this behavior by the Egyptians, could not make any sense of it. "But hey," she thought, "who cares why? This is fantastic!"

Julia also found that the Israelites and Egyptians bonded over their mutual dislike of Pharaoh. "Ramses is incompetent!" said an Egyptian artist to Julia during one such dialogue. "The hailstorm did it," he continued. "The public opinion is that Pharaoh needs to let the Israelites go. Your God is clearly more powerful than our gods. But Ramses is stubborn as can be. It has become a matter of wills; Ramses wants to show that he and his gods are more powerful than Moses and his God. How arrogant can you be? Clearly the winner is self-evident! Well, it can't be much longer now . . ."

Such proclamations by Egyptians were common. While life had gotten much better for the Israelites, it had become untenable for the Egyptians. Much money and property had been lost due to the plagues. No one was spared. Even the smartest, savviest, richest businessperson had sustained severe losses.

The pain and frustration of the Egyptians only became more widespread as the weeks continued to go by. Additional plagues came, with the ninth one being three days of darkness over Egypt. While not a physical harm, it broke the last will of the sane person. Yet, even with all of this Ramses was still obstinate.

Regardless, Hannah made it known that she was sure that even a person like Ramses would *have* to give in soon. One day, at about midmorning, as Julia and Hannah were drawing water from one of the wells, Lena approached them with the "I-know-something-important" look. "What is the news, Grandma?" Hannah asked.

Looking them both in the eyes, Lena stated in a voice of surety, "By this time next week we will be free and will be beyond the confines of Egypt."

Her words seemed to hang in the air. Hannah stared back at Lena as if she were in a trance. Then, as Julia watched Hannah's face, she saw a grin appear which then turned into a hopeful smile.

Suddenly, Julia saw Hannah's future life flash before her. She realized that Hannah could have a life! She could be an artist; she could rest; she didn't have to worry; she could finally meet some-one and have a real relationship. For the first time, Hannah's future was bright.

Over the next few days Julia saw this same hope spread throughout the Israelites like a breath of fresh air. Also, during these days, she saw the friendliness and generosity further in-crease from the Egyptians. She even got word that a good number of Egyptian families desired to go with the Israelites, wherever that may be. The Israelites accepted those that were genuinely inter-ested in going with them. Julia had experienced much so far in the journey, yet it was this that made Julia ponder greatly. Seeing the Israelites welcome the people that oppressed them amazed her. This was forgiveness; this was mercy; this was truly an act that could only occur with the grace of God.

After the passing of a further couple of days Goshen was packed, tenements were cleaned out, wagons were filled, and people were put into groups. Instructions came on how to prepare for their departure. The Egyptians who were coming with them brought everything they had and put it with the Israelites' property and materials.

It was the ninth day of the month, and Julia and Hannah were sitting at the table finishing breakfast. Hannah was telling Julia about all the ideas she had for how to decorate their new home but was interrupted when a neighbor came to the door and relayed, "Come on outside, one of the elders has a vital announcement."

Julia and Hannah went outside to a large crowd. In front of the crowd on a pedestal was one of the elders of the Israelites. The elder raised his hands, and the whole crowd fell silent, for they could tell by his demeanor that what he had to say was of utmost importance.

"My friends, I have come here on behalf of Moses, who him-self speaks on behalf of Almighty God. This night will be our last in Egypt, for when we see the setting sun tomorrow, we will see it from beyond the boundaries of Egypt as a free people."

The crowd then began to murmur in excitement. The elder then raised his hands again for silence. Julia could tell he had already given this same speech a few times today.

"Tonight will be the tenth and final sign, the one that will finally break the hardness of Pharaoh and cause him to let us go."

The elder's face then became solemn as he continued. "Tonight, at midnight, the Lord will come and strike down the firstborn of the Egyptians, person and animal alike. The Lord, however, will keep us safe; God will pass over us and such a fate will not touch us. As the signal for him to pass over, every Israelite will take a lamb, slaughter it, and apply its blood to both doorposts and the lintel of the dwelling they are in. This same lamb will be eaten for supper this night."

He paused. Julia kept her laser focus upon him as he continued. "We are now to be at the ready. For tonight's meal do not take time to leaven the bread; eat it unleavened. Yes, the herbs will be bitter, but there will be no time to prepare them. Have your traveling clothes on and keep your staff in hand."

The elder paused and let what he had just said sink in to the crowd. He then gave the last part of his speech. For this part, a smile came on his face and the tone of his voice became filled with excitement as he declared, "Tomorrow God will lead us home. Tomorrow we will be free. God bless you; praise be the God of Abraham!"

With that he bowed to the crowd and left. The whole crowd immediately erupted in talk. Happiness washed over Julia. She, Hannah, and all the Israelites were being rescued; the day was finally about to come!

Within an hour, the excitement turned to seriousness. All set immediately to procuring lambs, to do any final packing, and to be ready to go at a moment's notice. Every Israelite's residence and dwelling, for not a single one was missed, was painted with lambs' blood on the doorposts and lintel.

Just after sunset, Julia, Hannah, and Lena were standing outside. Hannah's father had literally inspected the house three times; yes, indeed, the blood was exactly where it should be. As the last vestiges of light left the sky, Julia, Hannah, and Lena took in the scene, each mesmerized by the significance of this time. They then walked into the house. Before closing the door, Lena scanned the room with her eyes. She counted her daughter and son-in-law, Jehu, Hannah, Julia, and herself. Upon seeing that everyone was inside and accounted for, she pulled the door shut. It locked with a click.

Chapter Eight

THE CALL

It was a sunny day in 1250 BC as Moses was shepherding his sheep in the land of Midian . . . That was all Justin could read of his open book before he felt himself being transported and the book disappear.

He now found himself in a pasture of varying levels of grass, some tall and some that had been consumed. All around him were sheep eating, bleating, some playing with each other. The day was indeed sunny, and a gentle breeze swept his face.

"I knew it was only a matter of time," said a man behind him with a sigh. "Gone missing, always wants to explore and gets lost in the process. Well at least it is early afternoon, and we have some time to find Runner."

Startled, Justin turned around toward the source of the voice. The man who was speaking to Justin was tall, had brown eyes, and had gray hair. He was the age of a grandfather, but strong and had a toughness about him. He wore a simple tunic of gray and brown. On his feet were sturdy but worn sandals. In his hand was a shepherd's staff made from deep brown wood. Justin figured it had to be Moses, whoever that was.

"All right, let's go and find that sheep," said Moses to Justin.

"What? Oh yes, of course, let's do that," answered Justin, who was trying to get his bearings while still being impressed by Moses, who seemed to have a larger-than-life quality.

As Justin surveyed the area, he saw a lot of land, tall grass, trees, and hills; not to mention that they were at the base of a mountain. Alas, with this terrain a sheep could be anywhere; this was going to take some time.

After some searching with no result, Moses turned to Justin and stated, "Most likely he went up into the mountain. We'll have to go up. At least he can't be that far up; he is a sheep, not a wolf."

After a while of searching the mountain to no avail, Justin stopped and yelled, "Moses, Runner could be anywhere. This could go on for hours. Let's get some help."

But instead of responding to Justin's question, Moses walked back towards him, pointed, and asked, "What do you make of that?"

They both began to walk in the direction Moses was pointing. Reaching a small hollow containing green grass and some leafy bushes, they stopped in their tracks. For in front of them was a bush on fire, emitting a soft but robust white light. "Incredible," said Moses softly. "This bush is on fire, but it isn't burning. There is no smoke nor ash."

Justin simply gaped at the bush. As he stood there, he felt a similar feeling as to when he was with the three persons in the forest. Then, to Justin's astonishment, he heard a voice, a deep and inviting voice that called out, "Moses! Moses!"

Moses looked at the bush and responded, "Here I am." There was a moment's pause, and then the same voice spoke again saying, "Do not come near! Remove your sandals from your feet, for the place where you stand is holy ground."

Moses stopped right where he was. On his face was a look of confused excitement. Before Moses or Justin could ask any questions, the voice continued, "I am the God of your fathers. I'm the God of Abraham, the God of Isaac, and the God of Jacob."

As Justin stood there in awe, a powerfulness almost too great to bear enveloped him, and, like Moses, he hid his face for he was afraid to look.

As God continued to speak to Moses, he said, "I have witnessed the affliction of my people in Egypt and have heard their cry for help. I know well what they are suffering and what they are going through. Therefore, I have come down to rescue them from the power of the Egyptians and lead them up from that land into a good and spacious land, a land flowing with milk and honey."

God then commanded, "Now, go! I am sending you to Pharaoh to bring my people, the Israelites, out of Egypt."

After moment, in a soft but determined voice Moses asked, "Who am I that I should go to Pharaoh and bring the Israelites out of Egypt?"

God answered in a voice of knowing and understanding, "I will be with you. This burning bush will be your sign that I have sent you."

Justin watched as Moses responded to God. "But if I go to the Israelites and say, 'The God of your ancestors sent me to you,' then they're going to ask, 'What is his name?' What should I tell them?"

God replied, "I am who I am. Tell the Israelites that I AM sent me to you."

There was a pause, and before Justin could even consider what in the world "I AM" was supposed to mean, God spoke further to Moses. "This is what you will say to the Israelites: 'The Lord, the God of your ancestors, the God of Abraham, the God of Isaac, and the God of Jacob, has sent me to you.' This is my name forever; this is my title for all generations."

Regarding how the rescue would occur, and how an obstinate Pharaoh would be convinced, God explained, "I will stretch out my hand and strike Egypt with wondrous deeds. After all such deeds have been done in their midst, he will let you go. I will even make the Egyptians well disposed toward the Israelite people so that, when you go, you will not go empty-handed."

Moses, who then became frightened at such a hard mission, told God that he was not an eloquent nor a good public speaker. In fact, he wasn't good at speaking in general because he often mumbled and didn't project.

To these concerns God answered that it was he who gave abilities and talents and that he would assist Moses' speaking abilities and teach him what to say.

God ended this dialogue in a gentle and reassuring voice with, "Take the shepherd's staff that you have in your hand. You will perform signs with it." As God said these final words, Justin saw what he could only describe as God's spirit come from the burning bush and rest on Moses.

After the dialogue ended, Justin and Moses remained for a little while in front of the burning bush watching and soaking up its divine glow. As Justin reflected on all that just happened, he felt that God wasn't speaking just to Moses but to himself as well. In fact, what he really felt was that God *had* called him to a similar mission. To what? That he could not place his finger on.

A while later Moses and Justin left the burning bush, put their sandals back on, and went down the mountain. As if by design, a little bit beyond the bottom of the mountain, was Runner. Upon finding him both Moses and Justin looked at each other and grinned, for they only took that particular path because of their encounter with God. "Well," said Moses, "it looks like God has already rescued at least one lost sheep through us!"

Thus, Moses, his wife, his sons, and daughters, along with Justin, went back to Egypt to complete the mission of rescue.

Justin, who had no knowledge of Julia's situation, spent the trip asking Moses many questions and listening to Moses' life story, which Justin found to be fascinating.

Moses explained to a captivated Justin that his biological father and mother were of the Israelite tribe of Levi. They married and had three children—his brother Aaron, his sister Miriam, and himself. The time he was born into was especially dark. King Seti, predecessor to the current Pharaoh Ramses, was having a fit of paranoia and had all the newborn Israelite infant boys killed, for he feared a rebellion. It was a massive slaughter, a crime that screeched out to heaven.

Upon knowing Seti's intentions, Moses' mother, seeing that her son was a strong and healthy baby, knew she had to send him away to keep him alive. When he was three months old and could no longer be kept a secret, she took a papyrus basket, made it watertight with a tar-type substance, and put him in it. She and

Moses' older sister Miriam then strategically placed it in the Nile River upstream of the palace so that the palace attendants would notice the basket when the current took it their way.

As the basket was floating down the river, Miriam stationed herself at a distance in the reeds and followed the basket to find out what would happen to her brother. As planned, it crossed the part of the Nile where Pharaoh's daughter, a princess of Egypt, normally bathed. As hoped, her attendants, as they walked along the bank of the Nile, noticed the basket among the reeds and fetched it to bring to the princess.

Upon opening it, the princess found a baby boy crying. She was moved with pity for him and knew by the dress and basket that it was an Israelite child. Regardless of his biological origin, this child became a son of the princess since she cared for him as her own. She named him Moses, for she said, "I drew him out of the water," which is the meaning of the name "Moses." Thus, he grew up as a prince of Egypt.

Moses' first memory was swimming in the Nile with his brother, who would also become his best friend, Ramses II. Moses grew to have many happy childhood memories of playing in the palace, finding different fish in the Nile, and being doted upon by the palace staff.

Adolescence came, and with it, admiration, not just because he was handsome, but because he was kindhearted. Moses also excelled in schooling, especially in the engineering disciplines.

His favorite memories out of everything were his times and stories with Ramses. They learned together and had their first hunt together. They got into trouble more than once but always found a way out.

As young adulthood dawned, they both became leaders in their own right. They led together, built together, and completed architectural marvels. They were two princes making their mark on history.

Life was good, Ramses was happy, and Moses was happy. Yet, that happiness was not to last, for things eventually fell apart. Why they did so was a question Moses had pondered for four decades, one in which he didn't have a clue as to the answer, that is, until now.

What happened to make life fall apart was this. Moses had never been a fan of the system of having the Israelites in bondage and neither was Ramses. They even admitted to each other privately when they were teenagers that it was unfair and that if ever they were in charge they would change the system.

As time went by, especially as Moses got older and became in charge of much, he saw the day-to-day hardship, brutality, and despair that was thrust upon the Israelites by the Egyptians. Over time, a slow anger increased inside him. For by this time, even though the story was officially classified, he knew of his birth story and that his origins were of Israelite lineage.

One day, while walking from a worksite back to the palace, he witnessed an argument between an Egyptian guard and an Israelite. It escalated in front of his eyes and the guard started striking the Israelite with his rod, causing the Israelite to give yelps of pain. Whether it was because he had a difficult day, or because his anger at the bondage hit a boiling point, Moses snapped, pulled out his sword, and struck down the Egyptian who was beating the Israelite.

Moses didn't mean to kill him, for he intended to use the flat of his sword. However, as usually happens in anger, intentions never become reality.

Moses attempted to cover the incident up, but the word got out. Pharaoh, that is Seti, was furious. Seti took it as a personal insult of the greatest scale. Still holding his paranoia about an Israelite rebellion, Seti accused Moses of being part of a conspiracy.

All these considerations made Seti desire the death of Moses. It was Ramses who ran enough interference so that Moses could escape.

It was at this time that Moses fled to Midian. There, he set up a new life for himself. He married into one of the clans and became a member of their family. He and his wife had children, and he lived the life of a well-off country shepherd.

Decades went by and there were many times Moses thought about the past. One of the acts he did in those years was repent of his killing of the Egyptian and made his penance before God. It was also during these years that Seti died, and Ramses II became pharaoh of Egypt.

Even before the burning bush, Moses felt that God had put it into his heart that he was being called to do something to help his fellow Israelites. Hence, by the time of the burning bush, Moses was predisposed to God's calling.

"And here we are now, about to go back to Egypt and see what course all of this history will flow to," said Moses as he finished telling Justin the story of his life.

Once they reached Egypt, things happened quickly. Moses told his brother Aaron and the elders all about God's plan. Justin was surprised how easily they accepted Moses' testimony. It was either a show of great faith or a sign of desperation. Probably a bit of both, he thought.

Thus, Moses, Aaron, and some of the elders went to Pharaoh and told him that the God of Abraham has commanded him to the let the Israelites go. The meeting did not go as intended because it struck a chord in Pharaoh's pride. Pharaoh refused, and even commanded the straw ration be canceled to make the brickmaking that much harder.

"A catastrophe!" yelled Aaron to Moses when they got back from the meeting. "Here we are, wielding the power of God, and what happens? Not only did Pharaoh refuse, but now life is twice as hard for us as it was before. Our own people are going to disown us!"

"Brother, God had already told me that Pharaoh would not believe at first," said Moses to Aaron. "Next time we go to Pharaoh God will accompany us with a sign. Will that be the end? No, but it will be another step on the road to freedom. All good things, even divine things, take time, effort, and patience. Who are we to judge the mystery of God?"

Moses went back to Pharaoh several days later. This time, by the power of God, Moses threw his staff on the floor, and it turned into a serpent. While Justin was freaked out, Pharaoh was non-plussed. Pharaoh then commanded his magicians to do the same, which they did (via smoke and mirrors). Regardless of the fact that Moses' serpent swallowed up the two snakes from his magicians, Pharaoh refused to let anyone go.

Over the next month, Justin witnessed the same nine plagues befall the Egyptians that Julia had. Before and after each came a warning from Moses to Ramses, a warning which he always refused. At times Justin thought it seemed like Pharaoh was going to let the Israelites go. For during the plagues themselves Pharaoh and his executives would be frightened and appear to make up their minds to let the Israelites go. Still, as soon as each respective plague passed, their stubbornness, pride, and arrogance got the better of them.

At midmorning on the ninth day of the month Justin walked side by side with Moses through the palace of Pharaoh. As Justin admired the vibrant colors, expert craftsmanship, and beautiful artistry, he found it hard to believe that a people as advanced as the Egyptians could treat the Israelites as poorly as they had.

"I have two prayers," said Moses to Justin. "The first is that my people will be freed; the second, that Ramses and I can make up and be brothers again."

As they continued to walk silently together through the palace halls, Justin could feel the immense gravity of the moment. He also felt great empathy with Moses. He really hoped that both of Moses' prayers would come true.

Justin and Moses then came to the ornate doorway to the great hall of Pharaoh's court. The archway and the room were painted with artistry and hieroglyphics that chronicled the accomplishments of the Egyptian kings of old. The light from the lamps flickered off the pastel paints, polished statues, and the glossy floor. The throne of Pharaoh, plated with gold and attractively painted, stood regally in the center of the room. Its ruler was not on it, nor was there anyone else in the room, nor was the great hall Moses' destination. Rather, he was to meet Ramses in his study for a private conversation.

Moses said a quiet prayer, straightened up, and walked swiftly with Justin across the hall into Pharaoh's study where Ramses was waiting for him. Moses opened his mouth to speak, but was interrupted by Ramses who, with a hint of thoughtfulness in his voice, asked, "Remember when you set me up with Nefertari for the Ceremony of the New Sun?"

Moses abruptly paused. This question caught him off guard. Nefertari was Ramses' wife, with whom he had multiple children, including his firstborn son. The Ceremony of the New Sun was an annual festival that included a banquet and a dance. They were sixteen and Ramses, being the crown prince, needed a date, but was turned down by another and was too afraid to ask anyone else. So, Moses told Ramses and Nefertari that each had asked the other to the ceremony. It took them an hour to figure out the whole thing was a connivance of Moses.

Recollecting himself, Moses gave a smirk and replied, "Yes, I remember it distinctly. I saved you that night."

At this Ramses gave a small smile. "Why can't life be was like it was in the good old days?" Ramses replied to Moses.

Moses then looked Ramses in the eyes and spoke. "Ramses, obey God; let the Israelites go. Everyone has had enough. You would be a hero to your people. I don't pretend to tell you that reconstituting your labor force by fair means will be easy, but it can be done. In the end it's a win-win: people would be fairly employed and there would be no fear of resentment or a rebellion. Seti lived in a prison of fear of his own making all his life—not a state you want to be in. We *can* bring back the good old days; with God we can do anything."

Ramses was deep in consideration and Justin could tell he was a man at a tipping point. Within that moment Justin saw in the eyes of Ramses a softening and a longing. All was silent; even the air hung in anticipation. If only Ramses would desire reconciliation too!

However, the small smile that was upon Ramses' face vanished. He then spoke. "You must think me heartless, yet, you know how life works. Egypt has always used indentured labor. How many people have been fed because of better irrigation? How many families have been given shelter because of the building projects? The list goes on."

"Yes," replied Moses, "I know how to run a state, but is a state really a state if built upon the backs of those in bondage? Is a state really good if only part of the population matters and is afforded dignity? Is a state of any worth if does not further the common good of all its subjects?"

At that Ramses' eyes narrowed as he interjected, "Is a brother and a best friend any good if he and his God send plagues that ravage tens of thousands of people and countless acres of land?"

Justin's heart sank and a feeling of sadness and bitterness crept through him. He saw that Moses had truly tried and had given Ramses every chance. God had given Ramses every chance too. Moses, too, could see that Ramses was not going to reconcile and that his arrogance and pride were to be his doom. An anger filled Moses, an anger at the fact that Ramses had thrown away everything, that because of his obstinance many would die that did not have to, and at the fact that he lost a brother and a friend.

Moses paused and took a moment of silent preparation. Then, standing up straight to his full height, he looked square in the eyes of Ramses and spoke in a voice of command. "Thus says the Lord: About midnight tonight God will go forth through Egypt. Every firstborn in the land of Egypt will die, from the firstborn of you, Ramses, to the firstborn of the simple laborer at the hand mill, as well as all the firstborn of the animals. Then there will be loud wailing throughout the land of Egypt, such as has never been, nor will ever be again. But among all the Israelites, among human beings and animals alike, not even a dog will growl, so that you may know that the Lord distinguishes between Egypt and Israel. All these servants of yours will then come to me and bow down saying, 'Leave, you and all your followers!'"

These words of Moses seemed to shake the very ground they stood on. Ramses glared back in silence at Moses. Justin could see that their roles were reversed; it was Moses who was a king, who had true power, and it was Ramses who was a slave, a slave to fear, to cowardice, to pride. For a split second their eyes met in a duel of wills, for even now Ramses could repent, but he did not. Moses stared back at him, turned, and Justin followed as he violently walked away.

Late at night on that same day, Justin joined Moses and the others of his household as they ate a meal of unleavened bread, hastily cooked lamb, and bitter herbs.

As midnight came, events beyond Justin's comprehension occurred. As God had said, the firstborn of all the Egyptians, persons and animals alike, were struck down.

That very same night Ramses II, son of Seti, the pharaoh of Egypt, the ruler of the most powerful and advanced nation-state of the day, summoned Moses. Ramses finally decreed what Moses and all of the Israelites had been waiting to hear for so long, that effective presently, all the Israelites were free and that they were to depart immediately.

Chapter Nine

A VERY INTERESTING TREK

THE RISING SUN ANNOUNCED the good news from heaven. As its colorful hues blanketed the earth, Julia and Hannah stepped out of their dwelling into the young morning air. They, as had all the rest of the Israelites, had gotten word that Pharaoh had let them go. Julia could not help smiling as she watched the look of delight on Hannah's face.

After all was ready to go, Julia and Hannah found themselves together in the biggest caravan the world had ever known. For something so big, Julia thought it was surprisingly well organized. Then, Julia heard the call, and the caravan took their first steps toward freedom. She walked past the tenements in Goshen which then opened up into the regular Egyptian territory. She then traveled past marketplaces, residences, and farms. Then the caravan followed a trade route, a route that had its origin far beyond the boundary of Egypt.

Of course, Julia had never been in such a caravan. It was interesting travel for one could go towards the front or the back and hang out with whoever they liked. As long as one was in the caravan, one could be where they wanted. People did just that; they visited friends and family, camped out with different people each night. It was like a massive reunion and road trip mixed together.

After a few days of travel through the open countryside, Hannah and Julia decided they wanted to make their way to the front of the caravan. Julia wanted to do this because she heard that God himself was their guide; that during the day he was a column of cloud and at night a column of fire. This, she had to see. It took nearly half a day to get to the front, given all the many people there were to say "hi" to and laugh with.

By dusk, Julia and Hannah had made it to the front of the caravan. Once there, they noticed a pleasant, soft glow. Julia saw that this glow of light was a column of fire—peaceful, gentle, and quiet like a cozy campfire in the form of a tower. It guided the Israelites like a moving lighthouse. As Julia looked upon such simple grandeur, she was wrapped in a blanket of peace and security.

As Julia stood staring at this site, she heard a familiar voice. "Julia!"

Julia immediately knew who it was and replied, "Justin!"

"Where have you been?" They both asked each other at once.

Julia replied, "I have been with Hannah and her family."

Justin responded, "I have been with Moses and his family."

Before Julia and Justin could tell each other about their experiences of late, Hannah, upon hearing Justin say "Moses," happily asked, "So, do we get to meet Moses now?"

"Yes," replied Justin. "Follow me." Julia and Hannah then met Moses, Aaron, and some of the core elders. Julia was more than impressed by Moses, and indeed, all of the praises she heard of him were certainly justified.

* * *

"What? It's been days and days since we left Egypt. One more trial? Are you sure?" asked Aaron quickly and gravely. Moses, Aaron, Miriam, and Joshua, along with Julia, Justin, and Hannah, were all together in the main tent.

"I will repeat," stated Moses. "Yesterday the Lord spoke to me that there is one more trial that we must endure, but it will truly be the final step of the process of our freedom from Egypt."

"And then?" inquired Aaron. Julia could tell by the tone of everyone's voices that there was a serious problem at hand.

Moses answered Aaron, saying, "The Lord has relayed to me that Pharaoh is going to make one last stand against us, and that the Egyptian army will come in force. But even so, there will be victory for us."

"What?" Julia whispered to Justin. "Is he kidding?"

Aaron then answered in words that matched Julia's thoughts as he said, "Moses, how can this be? Our whole Israelite caravan is at the shore of the Red Sea, at Baal-zephon, precisely where the Lord has instructed us to go. Since we are in the right place, how can this be a problem?"

Right place or not, if what Moses was saying was true, Julia could see it would be a very grave problem due to simple geography. The Egyptian army would be coming at them from the rear and the Red Sea was to their front. They would be trapped in the middle between the world's most powerful army and an immense sea of water.

Julia and the rest of those present simply stared at Moses. "We will have to sail or go the land route around the Red Sea. Neither will work. The land route would take weeks, and the sea route is not an option because we have no boats," said Aaron as he studied his map.

At that, Moses patted Aaron on the back and then walked away from the group. As Moses left to ponder, Aaron said to Julia and Hannah, "Well, I really hope Moses comes up with a good plan!"

Julia was relieved that there was no sign of any army that day or the day after. Thus, the caravan spent these days at rest, for Moses and the elders had not yet made public the final trial with the Egyptian army. On the third day of the rest, in midmorning, Moses, Julia, Justin, and the others were in council together. Moses had explained that today would be the day the Egyptians would arrive, but that this day would also be the final act in the greatest rescue in the history of the world.

The mood became tense, and all were on the lookout. Then, as Julia looked away from the Red Sea, back toward the direction of Egypt, she saw it. Coming closer was a herd of shining metal gleaming in the distance. It was quickly getting closer, and closer, and closer. At the sight of the Egyptian army the caravan erupted in worry.

"It's the Egyptians!" the people cried. Some started complaining and others grabbed swords. Men and women then went straight to Moses in anger and bewilderment, saying things like "We left Egypt only to die in the wilderness at some sea?" "If we were in Egypt, we would not have to be dying!"

Julia noticed one louder voice who shouted, "Clearly we are going to die; the Egyptian army is to our back and the sea is to our front!"

Upon hearing the commotion, the elders went around and began to calm people and let them know that there was indeed a plan. This only slightly helped matters. The minutes ticked by, and the Egyptians were moving surprisingly fast. Julia could now hear the Egyptian trumpets and see the hundreds of chariots complete with the shining metal of spears and swords. She also saw many on horseback.

The Israelite people continued to turn to Moses, giving him desperate looks about what to do next. Finally, Moses moved to the center of the crowd, stood on a rock, and looked at his people with full confidence. He then addressed them in a calm voice with authority stating, "The Lord God has rescued us from Egypt. He has kept his covenant with Abraham. Now you will see the final wonder, a wonder that will be remembered throughout the land and for all time, a wonder that will stand as a permanent reminder that our Lord is God!"

As these words echoed across the caravan, the cloud manifesting God that was in front of them, which was upon the shore of the Red Sea, moved and created a barrier between the back of the Israelite caravan and the front of the Egyptian army.

The Egyptians, still moving at full speed, pulled up in front of the cloud of God. Julia and the Israelites watched as the commanders of the army became prudently cautious and halted their attack. Pharaoh, however, had a mad look in his eyes and ordered spears to be thrown in the cloud. Spears were thrown, but such an exercise was useless. The Egyptian army plainly could not pass. Night came, and the cloud of God took its usual form as the column of fire, still acting as an impenetrable shield between the Israelites and the Egyptians.

During the night there was a lull in the action. Both camps, Egyptians and Israelites alike, did not move save for one: Moses. Quietly, at the command of God, Moses stretched out his arms over the Red Sea. As he did so a strong east wind sent by God came upon the sea, and it started to part.

As the first glimmer of dawn appeared the next day, Julia got up and gazed at her surroundings and found the sight surreal. For looking in a line from north to south she saw a great and powerful army, followed by a divine column of fire, then a massive camp of Israelites, and finally the Red Sea itself.

Julia could hardly believe her eyes as they fell on the Red Sea. The surface of it was no longer flat. The whole sea looked like a valley with lower, shallower water in the center and higher, deeper water to the left and the right. The parting of the sea, which began overnight with the east wind sent by God, was nearing completion.

Julia then got Justin and Hannah, who had reactions of astonishment just as she did. As the three of them looked upon the Red Sea with Moses standing at its shore, Julia felt a strong gust of wind filled with divine power coming from the east. At this, beginning where Moses stood, the water of the Red Sea fully parted in a swish of torrents of blue water and white foam. At the fullness of the parting, in the center of the sea, stood a wide path of brown dry earth that ran hundreds of feet below its surface.

As the light of dawn continued to brighten, Moses commanded the whole Israelite camp, "Now my friends, in the name of the God of Abraham, let us complete our journey to freedom!"

His voice reverberated throughout the camp, the people were fortified, and the Spirit of God was with them. Moses then turned and entered the path of dry land through the Red Sea. He was followed by the elders, and then the rest of the caravan began in tow. Julia, Justin, and Hannah walked in the front of the caravan with Moses.

Julia was astonished beyond belief as she strode across the floor of the Red Sea. What did it look and sound like? The path was wide, very wide, wide enough for the whole caravan with all the people, animals, and property. The greenish-blue walls of water looked like the surface of a lake rippled by a calm breeze. The water made barely any sound. High above was a new, dark blue sky with the hints of colors that preceded the rising of the sun.

What Julia remembered most was that there was no fear. In fact, there was a sense of peace and security. This was the final road to freedom.

The caravan continued quickly but calmly along the path. As it did so, more rays of light shown from the breaking dawn. Julia, Justin, and Hannah then came up the other side, and there in front of them as they came out on the other side of the sea was dry land. As the sun rose that day the last of the people of the caravan came up out of the path in the sea.

Moments later, right after the sun had risen and all the Israelites were accounted for, Moses stretched his hand over the sea. As he did so, the east wind stopped, the walls of water splashed down upon each other, and the sea went back to normal.

Being up front, what Julia did not see, but what those toward the back did, was the charging of Pharaoh's army. It was a futile escapade. There was never any real danger to any Israelite person, animal, or property, yet the whole army was in the path on the seafloor when Moses stretched out his hands, and, thus, the sea closed upon them. That morning all the Egyptian army that was sent after the Israelites perished. The sole survivor was Ramses II, for in the closure a wave took him back to the Egyptian side of the sea.

Neither Pharaoh nor Egypt would ever trouble the Israelites again.

The Israelite caravan took a rest at the edge of the other side of the Red Sea as all persons caught their collective breath. The sun was now rising, the sky was blue, and a gentle breeze of freshness fell upon them. Julia noticed that even the land was nicer and contained green grass and lively shrubs.

Julia could see that Hannah was in a dream. Hannah said afterwards that she could never explain how she felt in a way that could do it justice. The best she ever described it to Julia was that the cheerfulness of that day was so great, it took time to experience. It was like the lighting of a campfire; it started with a spark, then a small kindling, and then it grew to a magnificent light.

As the caravan began again under a deep blue sky, with delight beyond imagining, Moses and all the Israelite caravan—Julia, Justin, and Hannah included—sang this song of thanksgiving to the Lord:

I will sing to the Lord, for he is gloriously triumphant; horse and chariot he has cast into the sea. My strength and my refuge is the Lord, and he has become my savior. This is my God, I praise him; the God of my father, I extol him. The Lord is a warrior, Lord is his name!

Your right hand, O Lord, magnificent in power, your right hand, O Lord, shattered the enemy. At the blast of your nostrils the waters piled up, the flowing waters stood like a mound, the flood waters foamed in the midst of the sea.

Who is like you among the gods, O Lord? Who is like you, magnificent among the holy ones? Awe-inspiring in deeds of renown and worker of wonders. In your love you led the people you redeemed; in your strength you guided them to your holy dwelling.

May the Lord reign forever and ever!

Julia, Justin, and Hannah found the rest of Hannah's family, and they all met up. This gave Julia and Justin a chance to be together alone. As she walked with Justin, they each recounted the experience they had over the past few months. Julia told Justin all that happened with Hannah and her family. Justin explained to Julia all that happened with Moses, starting with Midian.

As the great caravan of the Israelite people continued its voyage, Julia found these first few days after the crossing of the Red Sea to be wonderful. Laughter was the music, and the glow of the newfound freedom was the rule. Hannah was positively giddy, and Julia felt extremely happy for her.

Like anything though, their travel wasn't magic, and there was some turbulence throughout the way. Issues one would expect with a crowd so big going through an arid region cropped up. However, God took care of everyone and provided water, food, and all the necessary logistics to go forward. The direction of travel was southeast, taking them from the Red Sea to Shur, then from Shur to Marah, then from Marah to Elim. Julia especially remembered Elim because it had the most refreshing springs of cold, clear water.

On the fifteenth day of the second month after the Israelites' departure from the land of Egypt (a month from the day they departed Egypt), they reached the territory of Sin, which was part of the region of Sinai. The region of Sinai was a vast track of open land of hundreds of miles, a wilderness of grass and shrubs untamed by humankind. It was in this southern part of the wilderness where Mt. Sinai stood, which was their eventual destination.

From Sin they went forward to Rephidim. Once there, they camped and took a break. The livestock had time to graze, repairs were made to wagons and carriages, and new clothing and footwear were fashioned. The break was indeed well deserved, and Julia was refreshed when the caravan again set out.

It was on the first day of the third month after the Israelites' departure from the land of Egypt that they came to Mt. Sinai itself. It was an impressive and picturesque mountain, one of the highest in the land. It was at the grand base of this mountain that the whole Israelite people made their semipermanent home.

For a few days Julia and Justin stayed with Hannah and her family in one of the many tents that turned the base of the mountain into a tent city. While many descriptions and observations could be made, the most important one, and the one that the people cared about, was that the future had potential and opportunity.

On one especially nice day, Hannah, Julia, Justin, Jehu, and Lena all walked a bit of a ways up Mt. Sinai. As Julia looked out at the tent city, the herds of livestock, and the beginnings of newly cleared farmland, Julia felt great admiration and excitement for this people. Here the people of Abraham and Sarah were being reborn in front of her very eyes.

As she sat pondering all of this while looking out at the scenery, Julia could then feel that their time at this part of the journey was almost up. In a sense, she had forgotten that she was on this special "journey." She was sad to leave her new friend Hannah; she wanted to see all that Hannah, Jehu, Lena, and the rest of their family would become.

"As strange as it sounds, I am going to miss all of this I think," mused Julia to Justin.

Justin gave a knowing look, put his hand on her shoulder, and replied, "I know what you mean. I feel invested too; I mean, look what just happened. We just saw God answer the prayers of his people and make the impossible happen. I feel connected to these people too."

As if on cue, both books entitled *Midian* and *Goshen* presented themselves on the grassy ground next to them. A moment after their opening, both found themselves back in the forest library.

Julia, with Justin, found Mary already sitting at the center table sipping a steaming cup of tea. A soft sunlight washed the room and was very conducive to allowing Julia to process all that she had just observed.

"So, tell me about it," said Mary. Julia then shared with Mary all that they had done and seen during the events of the great exodus. Justin then added the parts that only he saw from his perspective. Julia found herself excited to share and that such an event ought to be shouted out to the whole world. What amazed Julia the most was that God truly did the impossible, for without God's hand there would have been no way that such a course of action could have occurred.

Julia now wondered what was next and asked as much. Mary smiled and answered, "Indeed, you have just witnessed the greatest rescue of all time. Yet, you have only witnessed a part of such a rescue. The other part of this was the significant evolution in God's covenant with Abraham and Sarah, for from this came a path for the forgiveness of sins, redemption, and a way of life to live according to the beauty of God."

Chapter Ten

THE TOUR

STANDING UP, JULIA TURNED to go in the direction of the bookshelves. Instead, Mary led Julia along with Justin out of the door of the library. As the three of them stepped over the threshold to go outdoors, they did not come into the usual field of plush grass but into the center of a lively city.

"We are in Jerusalem in 955 BC, in the heart of the golden age of Israel of which many a song and story tell," said Mary with an asserted pride in her voice.

The first thing that Julia noticed was how new and clean everything looked. There were shops and government buildings. There were libraries and offices of all sorts. The city was spacious, had plenty of room for walking and for wagons and chariots. As a nice touch there were trees placed all around.

There were grand open-air markets with fresh vegetables and fruits. All sorts of items were for sale, arranged for viewing and exchange. Spices, colorful clothing, and tools of all sorts were for purchase. Some people were shopping, some eating with their friends, some just wandering around.

"Add cars, lights, and skyscrapers, and this could be any city back home," said Julia to Justin. In fact, disregarding the difference in technology, she was amazed at how similar everything was to present day. Deep down, people looked, talked, and acted the same way. This was a continuing discovery of the journey, that human nature really is the same throughout space and time.

After touring more of the city and having a delightful brunch at a restaurant, Julia, Justin, and Mary then went to the temple. It was a magnificent sight, for it was a whole complex rather than just a building. The temple was built of stone, gray and graceful. The roof was made of fine cedar beams, which had the perfect brownish-red hue. The windows were made with closed lattices, giving it a look of utmost importance.

In front of the temple was a large courtyard. Brick paths geometrically crisscrossed the courtyard and divided its well-kept green grass. There were manicured bushes and flowering plants throughout. Dotted around were benches for sitting. What brought everything together was that in the center of the courtyard stood a great circular stone pool filled with thousands of gallons of water. The sun reflected off the clear water giving it a spiritual component.

As Julia and Justin stood there taking in all the intricacies of the temple and its courtyard, a small crowd gathered near the pool of water. A man then came out of the temple who warmly greeted the crowd. Apparently, they were just in time for a tour, and he was to be their guide.

"What great weather we have for our tour today. God must have known you were coming!" he said in a jovial voice to which people laughed. "My name is Asher, and I am one of the Levite priests. Feel free to ask questions at any time, and if I start to talk too much, please interrupt me for that too," to which the crowd again chuckled. Julia instantly took a liking to him and knew that this was going to be a good tour.

"Let's begin," said Asher. "The temple was completed two years ago. It was built to replace the tent of worship, which had existed ever since the time of Moses three centuries ago. People come to the temple to experience the love and mercy of God, to make atonement for their sins, to praise God, to ask favors of God, and to come be with one another in community. And, if you can believe it, people even come to hear me preach!"

He then spoke about the courtyard and how all the flowers and artistic gardening were done to give it a spirit of reverence, and how all of this beauty gives a tangible sense of holiness. "For those of you wondering," Asher explained, "this pool is our source of water for our worship rites. The water is taken to be used for spiritual cleansing and for cleansing of the temple area after the animal offerings."

The group then turned to face the temple itself. Asher continued, "Now, can any of you tell me why the temple is built from east to west?" There was a pause from the crowd, then one woman raised her hand. "Yes, you, ma'am," said Asher.

The woman replied, "Is it to let the sunlight and fresh air in?"

"Very good answer," responded Asher. "Yes, two good practical reasons. To add to that, spiritually these are reminders that God is the light and that with him is always a new day. Beyond the practical reasons of having a regular current of fresh air, it does act as a reminder to us of the wind and spirit of God.

"Now let's take a look inside; follow me." The crowd then filed inside the temple, going first through the vestibule and then into the main part of the temple which was the nave. The walls had carved figures of cherubim, palm trees, and open flowers. The walls and floor were overlaid with gold. The roof's cedar rafters and their aromatic scent permeated the whole space, adding to the dignity of it.

"We are now in what is called the nave," explained Asher. "This is where we have our worship services and where the sacrifices take place." Asher then pointed to the large and ornate altar that naturally made itself the focus of one's eyes. He explained how it was here that the offerings were made to the Lord for a whole host of different types of prayers.

Asher then brought them to the end of the nave where there was another doorway. This entrance led to the holy of holies, the most sacred place of the temple.

"Before we discuss the holy of holies and the ark of the covenant," said Asher, "it would do well to review some history. For you historians in our group, you will love this. For those of you who are not so much into history, feel free to grab a snack and come back in two hours . . . kidding! Fifteen minutes . . ."

The crowd laughed and then all paid attention with fascination as Asher gave a history of the past three hundred years.

He explained that 1250 BC, the same year as the exodus and rescue from Egypt, was the year in which God, through Moses, enhanced the covenant with Abraham. The covenant came to include the Ten Commandments, as well as the other laws and regulations that the books of Genesis, Exodus, Leviticus, Numbers, and Deuteronomy record.

In 1210 BC the Israelites, after wandering for forty years in the desert, crossed the River Jordan into the promised land. There, they began their new status as a nation with their form of government being a confederacy of the twelve tribes, each tribe being named after a son of Israel, also called Jacob, a son of Isaac and grandson of Abraham.

Israel as a nation had its ups and downs, and growth took time. Over the next two centuries they would come to understand and enact all that the Mosaic covenant was supposed to do. During this time Israel was ruled by its judges and there was some success. However, during the second half of the 1000s BC, a time of corruption occurred as they were not doing a good job at keeping the covenant.

Hence, God sent them King Saul with the mission to unify Israel and bring a time of goodness. He accomplished this partially, but he himself did not keep God as his focus. It wasn't until God called David, son of Jesse, to be king that the good times of Israel came. Indeed, once King David was in full control, a golden age began and had been going on ever since. Israel was currently in a time of spiritual and temporal prosperity. Things had even gotten better under the current king, King Solomon, King David's son. It was King Solomon who built and dedicated the temple.

Asher ended his history lesson by stating that King Solomon was a descendant of Abraham himself. Julia couldn't remember all the names, but she did remember that the lineage included, from past to present and in that order, such figures as Abraham and Sarah, Isaac and Rebekah, Jacob and Leah, Judah, Zerah, Boaz and Ruth, Jesse, David, and Solomon. Asher pressed the important point that this lineage was eternal and would never be broken.

After Asher finished his lesson, he had the group make a semicircle around the doorway to the holy of holies and explained, "This right here, ladies and gentlemen, is the most sacred part of the temple, the holy of holies. As it is such a special place it is not open to the public. However, let me take you all through a guided tour through word and picture." At this, he turned, and with the help of an assistant, brought out three life-sized paintings of expert detail. Each was a picture of the inside of the holy of holies from different angles.

Asher then began his tutorial. "The room itself is made of fragrant cedar wood and plated with the finest gold. There, in the back center, stands the ark of the covenant which contains the Ten Commandments. The most important fact about the ark is that it is between the two cherubim on top of the cover of the ark, at the touching of their wings, where God himself dwells, all day and all night in every season of every year. The ark was built and dedicated three hundred years ago by Moses himself when the Israelites, our ancestors, were camped at Mt. Sinai. The construction of the ark . . ."

For whatever reason, the voice of Asher trailed off and Julia could hear no more. As she and Justin both gave each other a "what-is-going-on" look, she then saw that they were no longer with Mary, their group, or even in the temple. Instead, they found themselves on a mountaintop in a sort of open-roof hollow. There was a gentle wind, and under their feet was some small grass, pebbles, and dirt. Most interesting was that there was a yellow-golden haze about them.

"Where are we?" asked Justin.

"I don't know, but I don't mind being here," replied Julia.

"Yes, it actually is quite spiritual," Justin added.

Julia, after experiencing with Justin all she had so far, felt a friendship between her and him, and decided he was someone she could confide in. So she began, "It feels so strange. On the one hand, what we have experienced is amazing, seeing God do all of these acts, knowing that God really did create the world good, and so forth. It seems like it would be a 'no-brainer' to accept all that we have done. Yet it's like I feel like I have already tried accepting God and it didn't really work. Presently I find it hard to trust and I don't know why."

She took a second of silence and then continued, "If I am honest, I was on the edge of something that was not good at all, like I was about to make a terrible decision, or better said, I felt forced to make a cowardly decision. When I found myself in the forest it was possibly the greatest relief ever. Yet, I do not know what I was running from . . ."

Julia let her words trail off, and then looked intently into Justin's eyes. For a moment, she felt embarrassed for she just poured out her innermost thoughts. Justin then gave a laugh, not a laugh of ridicule but one of understanding. For he then explained that he, too, was sure he was coming from a situation similar to hers. And that, like her, he knew deep down that he was searching for a second chance.

After sharing such sentiments, with a look of earnestness Justin said to Julia, "I know for sure that what I am longing for is a second chance. Given the fact that we are here, doesn't that mean that God is giving us one?"

At these words Julia perceived at least a small sense of liberation. Yes, it had to be logically true. "And," went on Justin, "I also sense that this second chance is not just for us, but for many others as well. It is as though others depend on what comes of all of this."

As they talked and shared more, Julia couldn't help but wonder. They communicated so easily and so comfortably. Not only that, but she had found him to be quite handsome ever since they first met in the forest. Could it really be he was part of her second chance?

Julia's train of thought was interrupted, for she noticed a person coming up and around the bend. She didn't need any more details to tell her who he was. It was Moses. In his hands were two tablets. They were made of a granite of rich gray color with a glossy front and dark edges. They were blank and smooth.

Moses continued to walk and then stopped in the center of the hollow, the one in which Julia and Justin were in. Julia found that Moses couldn't see them for he was staring precisely in their direction without any notice of them.

Moses then stopped and stayed where he was. Next, as he turned his head to the heavens, as if on cue a light came through the clouds. It was a yellow-white light, gentle, warm, and not just of visible light but of love. With this light came the voice of the Lord—wondrous, powerful, and fatherly.

There, God gave ten commandments to Moses, which Julia recognized as the Ten Commandments that Asher had described. At the same time as God delivered them to Moses, God's spirit carved each in turn into the tablets, five commandments on each tablet. As Julia heard each commandment, she saw that each was a recipe for the restoration of Eden and a road map on how to participate in the covenant.

After God had written the Ten Commandments on the tablets, he gave Moses many other detailed laws that assisted in following them. These instructions regarded moral and ethical living, the nature of worship services, and specifications for the ark of the covenant.

God also gave laws regarding fair treatments of people, health, legalities, finance and business, and observance of the Sabbath. All in all, Julia counted the number of laws given by God to Moses to be 613.

After all of this had occurred, Moses picked up the inscribed tablets, which now had a sparkling quality to them, and then walked back down the mountain. As he walked, Julia saw that his face was radiant with the light and power of God.

Naturally and seamlessly, the scene then dissolved. Julia and Justin now found themselves in a large tent. It was dark outside, and she could tell that it was the peak of night. She found this tent was a workshop because there were tools, paints, precious metals, gemstones, scrolls, architectural drawings, and plums.

And there, in front of her and Justin, was the ark of the covenant. It rested on a purple cloth on a slate of granite. The ark was a rectangular vessel, three and a half feet long, two feet wide, and two feet high. It was made of the finest acacia wood. The inside and outside were plated with pure gold and a molding of gold was on top of it.

On the table next to it sat its cover which was made of pure gold. Just as Ashur had explained, on top of the cover were two cherubim of beaten gold, one at each end of the cover. Their wings were spread out above the cover with each wing touching the other at the midpoint of the cover horizontally. The faces of the two cherubs faced the center.

At each corner of the top of the ark were four gold rings. They held two poles of acacia wood that were plated with gold. These were there to allow the ark to be carried. Everything was perfectly polished, finished, and just right. It was a masterpiece of artistry. Julia surmised that the construction of the ark had just been completed, and it was now prepped for some sort of dedication ceremony.

Julia then stood above the ark and saw that inside it were the two tablets that she had just seen God make with Moses of the Ten Commandments. Each had the same sparkling quality as she had seen them have on the mountain with Moses. As Julia stood there in front of the ark, she felt a special peacefulness and serenity.

Then, after a time, Julia started to hear a faint voice of someone explaining something, which then became louder and clearer: "—took months for only the finest materials and most skilled artisans did the work, which was overseen directly by Moses himself."

She and Justin were now back with the tour group. Mary winked at her; Julia smirked back.

Asher went on, "Another question for you scholars out there: Can anyone tell me what type of stone the tablets of the Ten Commandments are made of?" A hand quickly shot up next to Julia and Justin; it was Mary. "Yes, please, to the lady in the blue," said Asher.

Mary replied, "On second thought I think I'll substitute my friend here; I am sure she can give a good answer," as she pointed to Julia. Asher and the crowd laughed.

However, without missing a beat Julia answered confidently. "The material is a granite of a rich gray color with a glossy front and dark edges. It also is said that they have a particularly sparkling type of quality."

Asher, a bit surprised, paused and then gave a smile of admiration. "Well someone clearly knows her history. Feel free to give the rest of the tour!" All chuckled and then Asher continued his talk.

After they had finished the tour of the inside, they were taken back outside to the courtyard. Asher focused their attention on the right of the temple entrance. There in bronze was the plaque of the dedication of the temple, which read, "The Temple of the Lord, the God of Abraham, Isaac, and Jacob. May he dwell here forever and may we his people always walk in his covenant with the Lord as our God and us as his people." Under this read, "Dedicated by the Lord's anointed servant, King Solomon, son of David, grandson of Jesse, 957 BC."

As Asher began to talk about the dedication of the temple, Mary turned to Julia and Justin and said, "One more time . . ." With that, the crowd around Julia and Justin grew into a packed courtyard. There in front of them was still the plaque, but shiny and brand new, which Julia figured meant it was now 957 BC, two years earlier. Next to it was a man wearing a crown of gold who had a regal stature. He also had the wisest of eyes. Around him stood other dignitaries, priests, royalty, and what looked like an expert architect.

The man in the crown was King Solomon, and they were at the ceremony of the dedication of the temple. Before Julia or Justin could say a word to one another in reaction, King Solomon raised his hands and immediate silence ensued.

All heads then turned to the center of the courtyard where there ran a long scarlet rug that found its terminus at the temple entrance. What came next was a procession led by the high priest.

He and his attendants carried the ark of the covenant through the courtyard to the inside of the temple to the holy of holies. As the procession passed by, Julia felt a sense of reverence.

What happened next was a most awe-inspiring sight. In front of the whole assembly of Israel, the cloud of the Spirit of God filled the temple. The crowd bowed their heads, and all took in this extraordinary moment. After a period of reverence, King Solomon raised his hands for attention. Then, standing before the whole of Israel, he stretched his hands toward heaven and recited this prayer:

> Lord, God of Israel, there is no God like you in heaven above or on earth below; you keep covenant and love toward your servants who walk before you with their whole heart. And now, Lord, God of Israel, keep toward your servant, David my father, what you promised: There shall never be wanting someone from the line of David to sit before you on the throne of Israel, provided that your descendants keep to their way, walking before you as they have. Thus, may you always hear the petitions of your people, us, whom you have set apart to be your heritage. Amen.

As King Solomon finished this prayer, people started to clap and cheer, and all raised their voices in shouts of praise to God for this wonderful day and all that it meant. Julia found herself shouting praises as well.

The applause around Julia and Justin continued, yet they saw the applause not of the whole assembly of Israel but of their tour group. The applause was directed at Asher. Julia, Justin, and Mary agreed, Asher had given an excellent tour and the three of them complimented him, for which he was thankful.

Refreshments were then served as the group mingled and people spoke to each other. Julia sipped her drink and looked around. What she saw was great progress in the fulfillment of the covenant that began with Abraham and upgraded with Moses, that after these three centuries, this Israelite people, who were now the great nation of Israel, were truly a holy people in a holy place. They were following the covenant, they loved God and neighbor, and they were prosperous both spiritually and temporally. Julia found that this was the closest she and Justin had been to Eden since Eden.

Mary then got up and motioned Julia and Justin to follow her. As they walked through the exit of the courtyard, they stepped not upon a street but upon the plush blue rug of the forest library.

Taking seats in the comfortable chairs, Julia wondered aloud, "While that was nice, and I do mean very nice, the problem of sin, evil, and death hasn't been solved. Also, Justin and I were speaking, and while we feel changed for the better, for which we are very grateful, all the questions we have about ourselves are just beginning to be solved."

Justin then added, "Indeed, and we also need to know who the other two godlike persons are, the one in the white and the one in the red."

On the heels of Justin's question, Julia asked, "By the way, you said that we were brought here to answer the prayers of others?"

Mary paused, looked both intently and lovingly in each of their eyes, and replied, "Indeed, there is so much more for you, as well as your calling to do great things for others. The many longings and questions you have will indeed by answered, even if in an unexpected way."

Mary took a moment and then continued, "As to answering the prayers of others, there are many more effects than can be counted, yet you, Julia, gave friendship to Hannah, which is exactly what was needed, and you, Justin, gave witness to others in your visible trust of Moses."

At that, Mary stood up and pulled a book off of one of the shelves. Its cover was of bright whites, blues, and golds, and as Mary brought the book toward them, Julia noticed its title: *Send Me*. Mary began to open the book and the same colors as its cover seemed to dance around. As this occurred, Julia remembered a seemingly long-lost hopefulness, not just for her but for a multitude of others. As Julia glimpsed this book come to life, she knew that the next part of their journey had begun.

www.ingramcontent.com/pod-product-compliance
Lightning Source LLC
Chambersburg PA
CBHW060439260626
47161CB00005B/1997